DEVIL'S BALLAST

Meg Caddy is a bookseller by day and a boarding-school tutor by night. Her first book, *Waer*, was shortlisted for the 2013 Text Prize and the 2017 CBCA Book Awards. She lives with two rescue cats and an ever-expanding bookshelf.

megcaddy.com

DEVIL'S BALLAST

MEG CADDY

TEXT PUBLISHING MELBOURNE AUSTRALIA

textpublishing.com.au

The Text Publishing Company
Swann House
22 William Street
Melbourne Victoria 3000
Australia

Published by The Text Publishing Company, 2019

Book design by Jessica Horrocks
Illustrations by iStock
Typeset in Caslon 11.75/16.75 by Duncan Blachford, Typography Studio
Map by Simon Barnard

Printed and bound in Australia by Griffin Press, part of Ovato, an accredited ISO/NZS 14001:2004 Environmental Management System printer

ISBN: 9781925773460 (paperback)
ISBN: 9781925774276 (ebook)

A catalogue record for this book is available from the National Library of Australia

*This book is dedicated to my cousin
(and feminist icon) Jessica.*

*(Sorry, Dad, you were in the running
right up until the fake shark attack.)*

Charles Town
(Charleston)

HOG ISLAND
(Paradise Island)

The Fort Potters Cay

NASSAU
(New Providence Island)

FLORIDA

Florida Keys

Eleuthera

Havana

BAHAMAS

ISLE OF PINES
(Isla de la Juventud)

CUBA

HISPANIOLA
(Haiti/Dominican Rep.) Carolina

JAMAICA

Port Royal

ANNE BONNY'S
CARIBBEAN

Maracaibo

Cartagena

PANAMA

N

1

BONNY

I counted fifteen dead men working the deck of the *Kingston.*

Well, they weren't dead yet, but the day was young and I had a full belt of shot.

I'd spent all day in the rigging, watching the other ship. She was a merchant vessel, fat with spice and silks, and though she had guns they wouldn't do her much good. Her crew didn't have our experience. Our hunger. The best the *Kingston* could do was run.

And our ship, the *Ranger,* was about to outrun her.

Men jostled and shoved around me, selecting hatchets and swords for the boarding party. I kept my head down, kept to the middle of the crowd. If the captain found me out it would all be over and I'd be picking oakum for a month. Dobbin, one of the other young hands, passed me an axe. If he knew I wasn't supposed to be there, he didn't comment.

Our sails clapped out and the breeze gathered behind them. We crested on a wave; spray danced across the deck. It was a warm day but the wind was up and the water was cold. I shifted my weight to stay upright. Just a few months before, the lurch of the ship had been enough to send me flying but I was a quick study and my balance had always been fair. Keeping my feet would be harder when we were fighting across the decks of the smaller ship, but I was ready.

The *Kingston* had been travelling at an easy pace. Now she gathered speed, and my heart skittered and rattled in my chest, beating out a gleeful chant of *too late, too late.* The *Ranger* was old and barnacle-studded, but she was fast. Isaac was a good helmsman and we were skilled hunters. Soon we would be hard on the *Kingston*'s stern. For any other ship we might have used the guns more, to cripple and capture. But the captain wanted this one for his own and he didn't want any damage done to her. If we used the guns, they'd be loaded with sangrenel and we'd be aiming to cut the crew to shreds with shrapnel. Strictly speaking, I should have been below, helping the gunners load up.

I glanced that way—towards the companionway.

No. I was not content to stay below in the sweat and swelter.

I jumped as two bony hands clapped down on my shoulders. Old Dad the carpenter leaned forward. His beard scratched my ear.

'If the captain sees you here he's going to turn blue, Andrew Bonny,' he said.

'So?' I asked, bracing myself to be sent below.

'So.' I could hear the grin in his voice. 'Don't let him see you. At least, not until the prize is won. And try not to get killed.'

I snorted and shrugged his dark hands off my shoulders. 'Good luck keeping pace with me, old man.' I turned away from him and kept my eyes ahead as we drew closer to the *Kingston*.

'Avast!'

I snapped around. Calico Jack was striding out across the deck towards us. His motley coat swirled about his knees and not for the first time, the sight of him made me catch my breath.

'Avast!' he said again as he joined us. 'Stop!' I stood behind Richard Corner but kept my eyes trained on the captain.

'Why?' One of the lads, Harwood, blurted out the question we all had in mind.

'Port Royal.' Calico's voice was tight. 'It's too close.

We'll be in plain sight as soon as we're around the point. We won't be able to catch the *Kingston* in time.'

The whole crew lurched with disappointment; silence stretched us thin. The balance of power on a ship was a fragile thing and, for a sick, wild, exciting moment, I thought they might mutiny. I saw it in their scowls, in the way their hands tightened on their weapons. And then, suddenly, the moment was gone. The tension slackened like a loose knot and the crew dispersed. Disappointment washed through me too—not at the lapsed mutiny, but the loss of the prize. I'd joined the crew with the expectation of loot and plunder, not a pursuit that fizzled out before a single shot was fired.

The *Kingston* crept away from us as the riggers started to bring in our sail. Isaac, on the helm, prepared to turn us away.

The crew accepted Calico's word.

I knew *I* should accept Calico's word.

'We're not that close to shore.'

Every head turned in my direction. I heard a disgusted noise that probably came from Isaac. Calico searched the crew and found me. His eyes narrowed.

I rushed on before he could reply. 'And we're fast enough that by the time someone comes to help the *Kingston*, we'll be away. Look at them, captain. They're easy pickings.'

'Are you questioning me Bonny?' Calico said.

'When did we last take a prize? When did we last finish a hunt?'

The crew parted for our captain. He grabbed me by the arm and hauled me towards the companionway. 'Don't push me,' he growled in my ear.

'Someone has to.' I wrenched my arm away and stood nose-to-nose with him. Out of the corner of my eye I could see other crewmen. They were going about their business but some lingered around us, trying to hear the conversation. I wasn't best loved on the *Ranger* and some of them obviously hoped Calico was going to give me a bollocking. 'Captain.' I lowered my voice. '*Calico.*'

'Don't. I weighed this decision before I made it. We don't know which ships are anchored in Port Royal. They could be upon us. And the port guns…'

'If we come in sight of the Port and there's a ship ready for us, we'll blast it to high heaven and then run. We've done it before. They won't be ready and we will.'

'You think it helps either of us if you call me out in front of the men?'

'Didn't you feel the tension, Jack? These men follow you because they believe you're braver than their *last* captain. They trust you to lead them into a charge and out again—with a prize.'

If it had been quieter, if we had been on land or out of sight, I would have kissed him then and he wouldn't have needed much more convincing.

I leaned back and shoved my hands in my pockets. 'You're not a coward, Jack.' I knew that would rile him. 'We won't have another chance like this for weeks. Now is the time. The winds are good, and God favours men of resolve.' I grinned and rounded my voice. 'He has given us the authority to tread on serpents and scorpions, and over all the power of the enemy, and nothing shall injure…'

'Enough.' He tried not to smile but I saw the tug of his lips. 'You talk more than anyone else I know.'

His blue eyes tracked over my shoulder, towards the *Kingston*. He raised his voice. 'You'll be picking oakum for a month, Bonny. Run your mouth at me like that again and I'll turn you over the side myself.'

'Aye, captain.' I tried to look humbled but I didn't have much experience in that.

'Loose the sails!' He shouldered past me and I turned and whooped. The crew scattered, reclaiming their weapons. Men moved through the rigging. And Calico was so busy pulling the crew together he didn't even notice me slipping back into the boarding party.

The *Kingston* tried to run. Her sails were still white and new and she glided out ahead of us for a short while. We surged after her, ragged and relentless. They had guns, but nothing mounted at the stern: they wouldn't have a chance to fire until we were alongside them. We just had to get over and spill some blood before they managed to ready their shot.

We drew along her starboard side just as we rounded the point. Our grappling hooks latched onto their railing and gunwale, splintering the wood. The merchants shouted and cursed, waving the odd weapon unconvincingly. They fired a gun but we were still at an angle and the shot cleared our bow by a few bare inches—then before they could fire again they had to wad and prime and reload, and wait for the right roll of the wave. We stole the time from between their teeth and flung ourselves onto their decks. Calico was the first one over.

If his resolve had been weak before, it was fixed now. He shot a man in the chest as I was scrabbling onto the railing of the *Ranger*. I stood there for a bare second. A wave surged under us and the ships knocked together, flinging a merchant between the vessels. I steadied myself and lept across, one foot on the gunwale of the *Kingston* and then both feet on the deck. Not enough space to swing the hatchet. The crew pressed forward, shouting and roaring. A merchant dropped to the ground with his hands in the air, begging. He was kicked to the deck and rolled away.

'Surrender!' Calico bellowed. His voice cracked across the deck and barely carried above our jubilant howls. 'Surrender and you *will not be harmed*!'

I strung my hatchet across my back, grabbed the black cloth I had fastened to my belt and ran to the rigging.

Someone came at me. I ducked. Old Dad grabbed the man around the chest and hauled him down, stabbing him in the gut.

'What're you doing?' he shouted as I grabbed a ratline and hauled myself into the rigging.

There were others up there but I knew I was faster than them. More men, probably the gunners, spilled up onto the deck from the belly of the *Kingston*. I counted maybe twenty merchants now.

As I climbed, the ropes rough under my hands, the wind replaced the acrid smell of smoke and powder. I was good at climbing, always had been, and though the tight bandages about my chest made it harder to breathe and the ship swayed, the mast swaying with it, I didn't slow. Someone started to climb towards me. An unarmed boy. I pulled out the gun from my left hip and pointed it at his face. I was a good shot. If he came any closer I wouldn't hesitate to fire.

'Climb down!' I shouted.

He was skinny and freckled, probably about my age, and smart enough to move away from me. Others followed him. My arms were straining and my hands were slippery with sweat by the time I reached the fork between the mast and the maingallant. I propped myself there, my fingers fumbling with the knots that secured the *Kingston*'s flag. It twisted and curled and fluttered into the ocean. Lost forever.

I secured our own flag. A black field; a skull above two crossed cutlasses. It snapped out in the wind. Beneath the sound of the waves and the wind, I heard a ragged cheer from our own crew. I grinned, breathless, and leaned against the mast. From where I perched I could see crow's nests and sails jutting out over the ridge of land. Then we rounded the point and Port Royal came into view. Everyone there would see our flag and know who we were.

Calico would be furious. Didn't matter. I *wanted* everyone to know. We were the crew of the *Ranger.* We were Calico Jack's people.

I wanted the whole damned ocean to be afraid.

2
BARNET

Jonathan Barnet stood on the jetty, supervising the loading of the *Albion*. He had selected this crew with care. They were hard men with a hard purpose. Men of God. Men of war. Some were new to his decks, and he watched them with particular interest. If they did not meet his standards during this voyage they would be put ashore without pay at the next port. There might be a flogging or two; it would stiffen the spines of the men remaining.

The Flemish hand Martin Read ambled past carrying a duffel. Barnet suspected Read would feel the lash on his broad shoulders before long. The man was quiet, but insolence lurked within.

'Step lively, Read,' Barnet said.

Read turned. His dark eyes were hooded, almost lazy. They flicked to a point behind Barnet, then back to his face.

'You have a visitor, sir,' he said. He went on his way.

'What?' Barnet demanded, turning to the stranger behind him.

The man was tall and angular. He might have been handsome on a good day but his shirt was sweat-stained and his unshaven face sported dark bruises. His breath reeked—Barnet found himself leaning back. He was used to the stink of men at sea, but a man on land had no excuse.

'Captain Jonathan Barnet? My name is James Bonny.'

'I am a busy man, Mister Bonny. What do you want?' If the man was looking for a job, he would find himself disappointed.

'I have come about the *Kingston*...'

Amusement prickled Barnet. 'You have come to commission me? I would have thought that several hundred pounds beyond you.'

'I'm representing a third party.' There was an edge to his smile. Barnet had adjudged him a drunkard, but now he reassessed. A merchant who had lost cargo on the *Kingston*?

'Speak, then.'

'I know the pirates who took her.'

'John Rackham and his men, yes.' Impatience flickered through Barnet's voice. 'Is that all you have to tell me?'

'I *know* them.' James Bonny leaned forward and ran his tongue across his lips. 'Calico Jack stole something from me. Something he still has in his possession.'

'So this *is* a commission.'

'This is ammunition.' Bonny drew a breath. 'You spoke before of Rackham's men. But it is not just men he keeps on that hell-bound ship.'

Barnet looked at him sharply. 'Yes?'

'When Calico Jack last departed Nassau he took a woman with him.' Hatred twisted Bonny's words, made his face ugly. 'Now she lives and works as one of his crew.'

'A woman pirate?' Fascination crawled in Barnet's chest.

James Bonny must have realised he had hooked his fish. He took half a step forward and dropped his voice. 'A woman. A pirate. A Delilah. Sent by the very Devil. I am sure she dresses as a man to deceive the rest of the crew.'

'How are you sure?'

Bonny's lip curled. 'Because she left dressed as a man, in the clothes she stole from me,' he said. 'The woman is my wife.'

'And you are going to pay me to retrieve her?'

'Think of it rather as an incentive on top of what

you will already be making. Word on the docks is that the merchants are going to commission you to recapture the *Kingston*.' Bonny handed over a full purse. Barnet checked the contents: more than the ragged man should have been able to afford. 'My wife's father is concerned for her welfare. As am I, naturally.' Sarcasm laced his tone. 'If you have the opportunity, we hope you will bring her back to my care rather than putting her in front of the law. If that is not possible, her capture and arrest will suffice. Mister Cormac and his connections will take it from there.'

'And if the merchants fail to offer me a commission?'

Bonny shrugged. 'I'm a gambling man. Call this my wager. And a gesture of good faith. My father-in-law is a wealthy man. There is more to come if you deliver his daughter to us.'

'You want her alive?'

'Oh, yes.'

Barnet scanned the other man's face. The capture of a female pirate would elevate him even above Robert Maynard, who had made his name slaying the notorious Blackbeard.

And while all pirates were, of course, an affront to God, a female pirate was a particular abomination.

'I will consider it,' he said, pocketing the purse. Bonny met his gaze and grinned. They both knew he had already decided.

3
BONNY

Calico, predictably, looked like God's rebuke to murder when I came back to the deck of the *Kingston*. The merchants were over the side in jolly-boats, starting their journey back to port. No ships were after us yet; it would take them time to supply and weigh anchor. Even then, we had a good wind and would soon be just two among the hundreds of ships tacking about the coast of Jamaica. We had already switched the skull-and-cutlasses to another flag. There was a variety to choose from, trophies of ships Calico and his men had taken in the past. They were useful when we wanted to be discreet. Old Dad had Noah Harwood over the side, taking out the wooden panel that sported the escutcheon. We'd flown our flag, but now it was time to slip quietly away from Port Royal before the merchants rallied and sent hunters after us.

Our crew set about moving the cargo and organising supplies. A skeleton crew could run *Ranger* while the rest worked the *Kingston*. She would be our flagship, our pride. The thought made my heart swell. This was the beginning of our fleet. So even as Calico stalked past and grabbed my scruff, I was grinning like a drunk.

'You just screamed our name to the whole of Port Royal!' he snarled.

'It's a good name.' I doubled my step to keep up with him. 'And now we have a good ship to match. Look at her, captain. She's beautiful!' I shrugged my way out of his grip. 'She's beautiful. We've been limping around on *Ranger* for months now. Living thin, living hard. This is the beginning of something bigger. Just look at Edward Teach! Say what you like about old Blackbeard, he took what he wanted.' And had held the seas in terror for his whole career.

'Edward Teach was a rapist and a madman, and now he's a dead man. Corner!'

Richard Corner, quartermaster and a helmsman, lumbered over to us. He was bearded and heavy-set, with big hands and an ugly face. I liked him, though he didn't have much time for my cheek.

'Bonny here is going to scrub every damned inch of this ship,' Calico told the quartermaster. 'If I find even a speck of blood by the time he's done, he's not getting paid any time this year. Keep two eyes on him, make sure he doesn't spare any effort.'

'Aye, Cap.'

'And *when you're done, Bonny,*' Calico went on, 'you can head back to the *Ranger*, because you're picking oakum in the brig until we reach Cuba.'

'What?' I didn't want to sit on the *Ranger* and pick apart old ropes. I wanted to sail on our beautiful new ship. The ship that had flown our flag.

'You defied me in front of the crew. You disobeyed my orders. You left your position with the gunners.'

'I'm quicker than half the men on this ship!'

'That's why you're with the gunners! Keep arguing with me and you'll be flogged.'

I knew he only said it for show but fear beat against my stomach when the words hit me. A small part of me remained curled up in the corner of a room, holding my arms over my head for protection. The thought flickered into anger. Calico opened his mouth and then closed it again. Maybe he knew he'd gone too far.

Then I shrugged and snatched a bucket out of Richard Corner's hands. Calico couldn't afford to call after me. The crew would ask questions.

I knew that would gnaw at him and I was glad of it.

He would have to make it up to me later.

Old Dad came to work alongside me, chuckling. 'You got him all riled now, boy.' He only had a few teeth left and they were baccy-yellow. 'When are you gonna learn to take orders?'

I dropped to my knees and started to scrub the decks with the stiff brush. 'When he gives better orders.'

'He's the captain. You'll have an easier life if you just do as you're told.'

'Easy is a little too close to dull.' I glanced at him. He was shirtless and skinny. I could count his ribs, and the raised scars that criss-crossed his dark back. 'Besides. You're the one who let me into the boarding party.'

Old Dad shrugged. 'I like you, boy, but you're stupid to question the captain. Especially in front of the crew.'

'Stupid, is it? I should pour this bucket over your head.'

He showed me all of his teeth. 'That would be even more stupid.'

He was old but he was wiry and quick. Richard Corner once told me he'd seen Old Dad kill a man using only a sextant. I had the good sense to keep the old fellow sweet.

'I like you too, old man,' I said.

'Of course you do. Now put your back into it, Bonny. Decks won't scrub themselves.'

My anger at Calico seeped away after three hours of scrubbing. I was too tired to hold a grudge. When I was done, I crossed to the *Ranger* to pick oakum in the brig as ordered. Truth told, I was glad of the smaller crew. Fewer people around, more chance to remove the bindings from my breasts and change my shirt to something looser. If I left the bandages too long, they dug red welts into my sides and made my chest ache.

Over the months at sea I had suffered in the crowd of the ship. Pirate crews almost always ran heavy for numbers in a fight. It meant there was less to do by way of chores, but also that there was no hope of privacy. That was difficult at the best of times. Almost impossible when I needed to change the bindings, or when my monthly courses were due, or when I wanted time with Calico.

The skeleton crew on the *Ranger* troubled me. Jimmy Dobbin and Noah Harwood were about my age. They weren't overly bright and they liked to scrap, but I could work my way around them. Richard Corner was a stout fellow with a stout heart. He told good stories and he half-liked it when I ran my mouth off at him. Sedlow and Isaac, however, were a different matter.

Isaac was one of the helmsmen. He was a big, broad man; like Old Dad, a former slave. Smart. Watchful. Calico's dearest friend. I didn't think he knew what I was, but not a day passed that I didn't feel his suspicious eyes on me. He was waiting for some sort of slip, and

I didn't know what he'd do if he caught one. He stood at the wheel the day after we took the *Kingston*, sweat gleaming off his deep brown skin. It was a hot day and we were the only two not to have stripped our shirts. I imagined that Isaac, too, had more than anyone's fair share of scars.

And Sedlow…I watched him out of the corner of my eye as he prowled the starboard side. Tall, lean. Not an ugly man, in low light, but mean. Mean like a boy drowning a kitten in a bag to feel its panic. Mean like my husband.

Sedlow had not come after me yet; not really. Just the odd shove or cuff about the head. But cruelty was graven in every line of his face. He was a man who liked to hurt just because he could. I couldn't tell, now, if he was pleased or angry to be on the *Ranger*. He'd been sent over as the second carpenter. It was an important role on any ship and though Old Dad was better, Sedlow could hold his own. If he was unhappy to be left here he would take it out on the smallest crewman aboard and that was me by a good half a head. If he was pleased, that didn't bode well either.

'Eyes down, Bonny.' Corner passed me. He had a coil of rope over his shoulder. 'Do your work. Don't start any fights.'

I shielded my eyes from the sun. 'Who said anything about fights?'

'I've known you for two months. Think I don't recognise when you're spoiling for one? Captain's rowing over soon to give us the charts. I want things running smooth when he arrives. So keep your eyes down, pick oakum, and just...Just.'

'Mister Corner, I don't know what you're talking about.'

'First week out with us, you called George Fetherstone a...what was it?'

'A bed-swerving fustilarian? That doesn't sound like something I'd say.'

'Your tongue is quicker than your wits, boy. And we both know which will serve you better.' He tossed my hair and went on his way, leaving me to my thoughts. I knew he was right but I had spent two voiceless years in Nassau. Now I couldn't seem to help myself when it came to saucing the other crewmen—especially those like Fetherstone, who acted like he had a ramrod permanently shoved up his arse.

The *Kingston* slowed and put down anchor. I feigned disinterest as they lowered a jolly-boat but my eyes tracked Calico when he came across to us. He always wore the patchwork coat for battle but it was a warm night and he was just in a shirt and breeches now. He looked less the captain and more the man. When he reached the *Ranger* he strolled across the deck, talking easily with his crew. He and Isaac clasped hands and laughed over some shared jest. I hunched my shoulders and concentrated on picking apart the old rope. The fibres would be mixed with tar and used to plug the space between the boards when the sea and the changing weather shrank the wood. It was hard work on the fingers, and dull besides. But right now I was glad of it.

'Bonny.'

I couldn't pretend I didn't hear him. He stood by his cabin, arms folded, watching me.

'Aye?'

He walked into his cabin, leaving the door open for me. I set my teeth, dropped my oakum into a bucket and trudged after him. Whether or not he lectured me, I could feel the eyes of the other crewmen. Their stare prickled and heated my skin. I stepped through Calico's door and closed it behind me. It was dark and cramped in there. Calico dressed like a patchwork king but he lived like a common man. There was a pallet, and a small table bolted to the deck. A chest in the corner, where he usually stowed his coat and what few valuables he didn't keep on his person. The cabin smelled of him: tar, smoke, brandy.

'Keep your voice low,' he said.

'I'm not an idiot.'

'Our flag on the mast of the *Kingston* says otherwise. What was the point?'

I shrugged. 'No sense in us having a fleet unless the ocean knows about it, Calico.'

'You made us a target.'

'We'll always be a target. Question is whether we slink in the shadows or fly our colours. I figured you'd want to fly our colours.'

'You figured wrong.'

'Is anyone following us?'

'Not yet. They'll come. We've outrun any followers so far but that can't last. You've put us all in danger.' He paused. 'And you cannot undermine me in front of the others.'

'Or what? You'll have me flogged? I may as well return to my husband.'

He winced. 'My words were for the crew's benefit.'

This was as close to an apology as I'd get. I folded my arms and leaned against the cabin wall.

'You know I'd never hurt you,' he went on.

'So you've said.'

Our eyes met. My stomach swooped. I dropped my gaze. I'd promised myself I wouldn't be a giddy fool around Calico Jack, but I couldn't help myself when he looked at me like that.

He took my hand and drew me to him. I didn't pull away.

'Why send me back to the *Ranger*?' I asked. 'I came to sea to be with you.' This was not entirely true. I'd had plenty of good reasons to leave Nassau. If Calico hadn't taken me aboard, I would have found another ship.

'You're distracting,' he said. 'Better for us to work on different ships, for now. And you'll have more space here to…it's safer for you without so many others around. But we're bound for Cuba, and we'll spend some time in the islands nearby. We'll find some excuse to be alone. Properly alone.' His lips brushed the corner of my mouth and I found I couldn't hold onto my irritation. Here, in Calico's cabin, was the only place I could relax, and be Annie instead of Andrew. A space between the world of corsets and the world of corsairs.

'And then what?' I asked. 'You'll make an honest woman of me?'

His soft laugh won me. 'I wouldn't dare.'

4
BONNY

Calico left before night fell. I felt lighter. Couldn't tell if it was relief that things were once more easy between us, or if I just felt hollow with his absence. Either way, I finished my meal and my tasks for the day and went to the rigging. It was my favourite part of the ship. When I was a child I liked to climb trees, a tiny buccaneer who stole birds' eggs and scared squirrels. At the time the canopy had felt like the crown of the world. Now the trees seemed tame compared to the sway and take of the rig. Each time a wave rolled beneath us, the mast tilted impossibly far—so far it seemed there could be no hope of coming back up again.

The larboard side was endless ocean. It shone as the sun started its descent. Above, the clouds mirrored the waves, starting in deep and rolling down towards us. The ridge of each cloud was tipped with white, pink, red, gold. I sat with my legs through the gaps in the rigging and rested my chin on a ratline. My arms dangled, elbows crooked in knotted corners. The rigging swung gently with a breeze.

I wasn't used to the quiet. As a child in Ireland I'd run riot with the local lads. Even when I was up in the trees I'd been causing trouble: pelting people with eggs, calling out insults, trying to escape bigger children. Later, in Charles Town, I'd fought and scrapped and slept my way out of my father's favour. And in Nassau...

I didn't want to think about Nassau but it crowded the peace out of my mind.

A small, cramped room. Thick, hot air. The taste of blood on my lips. No gun, no sword—only a half a board of wood, sharp where it had snapped off. My hands were raw and sore from prying it up. Every noise made me twitch. Couldn't leave. Couldn't stay.

He'd be home soon.

I closed my eyes and listened to the sound of the ocean. It whispered of freedom and revenge and when I opened my eyes the dark swelter of Nassau was far behind me.

'Bonny! Get down here!'

The sun was low. I must have slipped out of time. I glanced at the deck.

Sedlow was calling for me.

Watch yourself, Bonny, I told myself as I climbed down the rigging. I didn't rush. No need for him to think I was too eager to obey. I was cabin boy for the crew but that didn't mean he could get used to me jumping to attention every time he lifted his voice.

My feet found the deck.

'Here.' He shoved a bucket at me. 'Bilge pump's stuck.'

My lips turned. Usually a stuck pump meant there was a dead rat in it. I had no desire to go down to the bilge, the very deepest section of the ship where foul water and vermin gathered.

'Why are you giving it to me?' I asked. 'Bilge pump's your job today.'

'Do as you're told, boy.'

'Mister Corner gave me my own jobs, and I've done them all. Doesn't say anywhere in the Articles that I have to do your jobs too.' The Articles were the laws of the ship, signed by each man aboard.

Sedlow's face settled into a glare. He was bigger than me—but then, almost everyone was. He was built solid, too. A brawler. I knew he'd been a slaver before he signed on with Calico.

He grabbed my arm. Twisted it. Lowered his voice.

'You're getting cocky, boy,' he rasped. 'Think you're too good to do the work? Think you're better than us?'

I bit my tongue but a retort slipped out anyway. 'It's not that I've given it a lot of thought, to be honest.'

'Captain lets you have the run of things, don't he? Doesn't seem to matter how many times you go against his word. Why's that, I wonder?'

I pulled against his arm and he yanked me closer. His breath smelled of tobacco and tooth-rot. 'Maybe I know why,' he said. 'I'm thinking the captain's got a fancy for the cabin boy…'

I tensed my muscles, ready to move. Ready to drop the heavy wooden bucket on his foot and ram the heel of my palm into his nose. Spin when he released my arm, kick him in the crotch. Grab his head. Yank it into my knee. His hand tightened. I drew back my arm.

'Sedlow.'

Isaac was a big fellow but he moved real quiet. Sedlow's eyes latched onto him. In days past Isaac may have been a slave and Sedlow may have been a slaver. Here and now Isaac had a gun.

Sedlow knew better than to try his luck with Calico's right hand. He dropped my arm and spat on the deck. 'Boy can't take orders.'

'Depends who's giving them.' Isaac never raised his voice. He was still and relaxed now, his dark gaze unwavering on Sedlow's face. 'Aren't you supposed to be pumping the bilge?' A vein twitched at Sedlow's temple. I watched, enjoying the moment. Sedlow knew Isaac outranked him. More to the point, Isaac was capable of beating him senseless. I didn't imagine the sting of that knowledge would ever fade for Sedlow, who wheeled about and set off down the deck.

I glanced at Isaac, trying not to let my relief show.

'I should have let him clout you,' he growled. 'Might've stopped your mouth.'

'Possible but not probable. I had the situation in hand.'

'He's worth two of you!'

'Isaac, he's not even worth *one.*'

'He's going to be after you now. You know that. And the captain won't always be here to watch your back. Neither will I.' He lowered his voice. 'You know what your problem is, Bonny?'

'I do hope you're going to tell me.'

'Ship.'

It startled a laugh out of me. 'Ship? Isaac, are you addled?'

'No.' He grabbed my shoulder and spun me around. *'Ship.'*

There was a vessel to the stern. Not too close but gaining fast. In the new darkness I couldn't tell if her port lids were flipped but I knew she was big. A man-o-war. Her sails were just thin slivers of cloud to my eye, but enough to bring them after us at a good speed.

I muttered an oath. Our skeleton crew would be no match for another ship, especially not one of her size. The rest of the crew, ahead on the *Kingston,* couldn't come about and reach us in time. A firefight with the man-o-war would be our end. We'd be a cluster of sinking splinters in less than an hour.

If they were hunting us, our only chance was to run.

There was no time to raise a flag to warn the *Kingston.* Isaac ran the length of the ship. He reached the bow and leaned over so far I thought he might fall.

'Captain!'

We were close enough that one of the lads on the *Kingston* swung around when Isaac called. He went sprinting for Calico. Richard Corner grabbed my shoulder and shoved me away from the rail.

'Get on the swivel gun!' he shouted. 'Sedlow, you too. Dobbin, Harwood, up in the rigging!'

I skidded across the deck and dropped to my knees in front of the swivel gun. It was smaller than our other guns but it could do some hellish damage, and it was the only one that would do us any good here. We couldn't take a broadside from the other ship but we could fire the swivel from our stern, aiming at the bow of the ship behind us. It gave a small target area but if we were careful we might slow her down.

Sedlow pulled the swivel into position. I gripped the rail and swung myself almost out above the water to ram the shot and more wadding into the guns. The ocean gaped beneath me. My hands, slick with sweat, jumped on the rope as I slipped. I strained and pushed myself back onto the ship. We jammed an iron into a small touch-hole to break open the cartridge. I filtered more powder into the touch-hole and helped Sedlow mount the gun.

'Hold!' Corner commanded. 'Hold. Wait until captain gives us the signal.'

I didn't want to hold. Sedlow's breath was harsh and loud on the other side of the bore. I could feel my heartbeat not just in my chest but in my temples, through my throat, behind my eyes, in my fingertips. I wanted to *move*, but instead I braced my shoulder on the swivel gun and waited. I didn't recognise the other ship's colours, which meant it was unlikely she was a pirate or naval vessel. Now she was nearing I could make out faint ridges jutting out from her side. Her port lids were open. If she came alongside us, we'd be hit with volleys of shot.

I looked over my shoulder, towards our own bow. The *Kingston* sped ahead of us, sails all out. I told myself they'd never leave us behind. If this ship caught us, Calico would come back.

'What signal are we looking for?' I shouted.

The *Kingston* gave me my answer. Through the darkness I saw the skull-and-cutlasses flag rising on the mast: an act of defiance, a challenge. It felt like a love letter.

'Fire!' Corner shouted. Sedlow prepared to light the linstock as the prow dipped and we rose in the water.

'Wait,' I said. 'Wait!' We needed the right moment, but Sedlow ignored me. There was a small flash as the slow match lit; I jumped to the side. The swivel gun shot back, the sound punching right through me. My ears sang. I dragged my head up. A miss. The shot went into a wave, skipped once, and fell short.

'I told you to wait!' I snarled but my voice was tinny and hollow in my own ears and I couldn't tell if Sedlow heard me. There wasn't time to argue. We cleaned the bore, then wadded and primed the gun again. I rammed her and turned to Sedlow. He was already preparing to light again. I lunged across the hot bore and grabbed the linstock out of his hand.

'Red-headed Irish bastard!' he bellowed.

'Well, yes,' I muttered, readying the linstock as the waves turned the ship beneath us. I waited. Held my breath. Then the stock ignited and the flare of light was brilliant. Moments later the ship tipped again and the gun jolted back. I knew we'd hit before I even saw it. I sat back on my heels and cackled. Fire and smoke blazed the dark night and shimmered off the sharp waves.

The wind took in our sails and we pulled ahead while the ship on our tail struggled and smoked.

'Another!' roared Corner. Sedlow grabbed the linstock from me while I rammed the gun again. Whatever blow he struck or failed to strike now, we'd done enough damage to slow our hunters. The shot rang a third time, glancing off the starboard side of the other ship. A hit, but not a good one.

'That's enough!' Corner waved at me to get up. I scrambled to my feet and over to him. 'Help me jettison the ballast!'

'What?' I dug into my ear but it didn't do any good.

'We're going over a sandbar!'

Calico Jack liked his ships the way he liked his women—small, nimble, and preferably stolen. The *Ranger* and the *Kingston* both had a shallow draught; so long as they weren't hauling too much weight they'd clear a sandbar much more easily than any man-o-war. It would buy us precious time. I ran to the companionway and dropped to the lower decks. We pulled up barrels and ballast from the orlop, careful to balance it so we didn't upset the delicate harmony of the ship's motion. Then, with help from Sedlow, we hefted them over the side. Ahead of us, the *Kingston* skipped on through the water, almost scudding ahead of the wave. I could faintly make out the sandbar as they passed over it, the smooth flow of the water illuminated briefly by the ship's lanterns.

'Steady, Isaac,' Corner cautioned. Isaac's shoulders were bunched, his feet planted on the deck. He was an oak, somehow grown tall and strong in the midst of shifting soils. The enemy ship was dropping back fast now as they struggled to deal with their damaged bow. I leaned on the railing at the stern and watched her recede as we glided smoothly across the sandbar.

'Bloody brilliant,' I breathed. Then a surge of nausea hit me. I buckled and retched over the side of the ship.

5
BONNY

By morning the man-o-war had disappeared from sight, but Jim Dobbin and Noah Harwood pestered me about my battle-shakes long into the day. Dobbin and Harwood were the next two youngest on the ship, twenty-two and nineteen, so they enjoyed having someone younger and smaller to push around. They thought it a real tickler that I couldn't seem to keep anything down.

Isaac didn't find humour in the situation. He haunted the deck, standing silent on the helm with a troubled expression on his face.

'*What*, Isaac?' I asked. 'We won, they're nowhere to be seen, it was a great success. What's the problem?'

'I know those colours,' he said. 'I know them but I can't remember who sports them.'

'Does it matter?'

'It might.' He scraped a hand over his shaved head. It was a hot day already and tracks of sweat gleamed on his neck. 'You look like a kicked dog,' he added grudgingly. 'Go get some rest.'

I rolled my eyes.

'Any other man would leap at the opportunity for a shorter watch,' he said. 'And he wouldn't normally get it, not just for battle-shakes. But you did well last night. This is why the captain keeps you on the guns, Bonny. You've a good eye, an instinct for it.'

'I don't have battle-shakes. I've *never* had battle-shakes. It's just a bad stomach. Something I ate.'

But I wondered. I didn't know why I'd reacted that way to the chase. Maybe because for the first time, Calico hadn't been there to watch my back. I didn't want to rely on him like that. It felt like a weakness.

'Happens to everyone sooner or later. Nothing to be ashamed of. Go below and sleep.'

'It's nothing to be ashamed of when you're built like a house,' I retorted. 'I'm the smallest man here, Isaac. I can't afford to have people think I lose my stomach at every snap of arms. Besides, I'm not tired. I'm bored, actually.'

I *was* tired but more than anything I was anxious to stay out of Sedlow's way. He was down on the orlop deck taking stock of our supplies. Normally I wouldn't have minded starting a little something with him but not when I was feeling this way.

'So you want me to give you a job?' Isaac asked.

'Try me.'

'Go clean the heads.'

My eyebrows shot up. 'Was that a joke? Did you just make a joke about me cleaning the shit-holes? Well, hell, maybe they killed us last night after all and I've gone to heaven.'

'Let me be more clear. Go anywhere else, do anything else, bother *anyone* else.'

I glanced at the rigging. Dobbin and Harwood were up there, larking around. The thought of their humour made my head ache.

'I think I'll stay here,' I said. 'How long until we anchor?'

He sighed. 'Come here,' he said. I went to stand at his elbow. 'See those islands? Used to be turtle fishermen lived there. But there was some raid by the Spanish and the settlements are abandoned now. Mostly abandoned. Good place to stop and careen. We'll be there a few days, if captain says so.'

'Do we have enough food for that?'

'Depends. How do you feel about eating giant lizards?'

We dropped anchor in the snug bay of one of the islands. I itched to see Calico again, to find a quiet place and spend some time in his arms. It would give me a chance to get away from Sedlow, too. I felt that man's eyes on me all the way from the ship to the shore. He hadn't said a word to me since the night before. I had bested him twice, once about the bilge pump and then again on the guns. He wasn't going to forget it.

The men who had worked the *Kingston* came out to greet us: they had landed an hour or so before. They strode out onto the beach and helped to haul the jolly-boats, tying them off to rocks and trees as we exchanged tales of the night's pursuit.

'Who fired the second shot?' Old Dad asked.

'Harwood,' I replied, and grinned as everyone goggled at Harwood for a moment. '*Me*, you gulls. No one's going to let Harwood on the guns. He'd sink our own ship.'

'Brat.' Old Dad snorted and tossed my hair. 'You're a good shot though, Bonny. Saved our arses back there.'

'Yeah, except *then* he lost his dinner—'

I elbowed Harwood in the ribs before he could finish running his mouth in front of the whole crew. 'Except nothing,' I said, speaking over him. 'I'm a big damn hero. Where's the rum?'

'Keep Bonny away from the rum. He's bad enough sober.'

I shielded my eyes from the sun and watched as Calico strolled down the beach towards us. It always caught me by surprise, the way I found myself pulled towards him. I folded my arms and made myself hang back as the others flocked around him. The crew had their moments of malcontent but they *liked* Calico. He made them feel noticed. Stronger. Funnier.

I waited until there was a lull before I approached him. 'Captain.'

'Bonny.'

We didn't say anything more but I felt promise in the exchange. I grabbed my pack from the jolly-boat and took up a small barrel of salt under one arm. I wanted to walk beside Calico but he had Corner at one elbow and Isaac at the other. Instead I walked by Old Dad.

'You'll get extra pay for that shot,' he said. 'Corner's a good quartermaster and he believes in giving credit where it's due. Besides, captain will be happy to see Barnet eat some powder.'

'Who's Barnet?'

'The pirate hunter. That was his ship. No one told you?'

'No one knew. Isaac said he recognised the colours but he couldn't remember who they belonged to.'

Old Dad whistled between his teeth. 'Figures. Isaac's never been foul of Barnet before. When you've been around as long as I have, though, you'd know the *Albion* anywhere. Jonathan Barnet's her captain and he's a hard bastard. Loves King and Country, hates pirates. A gut-deep hate. He actually *asked* for the commission to hunt our like. I heard Edward Teach murdered his cousin.'

I snorted. 'Edward Teach has murdered everyone's cousin, if you believe what you hear.'

'Don't take it too light, boy. It was a fine thing to see Barnet take a hit but he'll be back on our arses at some point. I've known too many good hearts dancing the hempen jig. I like your pluck, but I'd hate to see you swinging from a gibbet because of it.'

'Have you been talking to Isaac?' I shrugged his hand off my shoulder. 'If Barnet comes after us again he'll get more of the same. I'm not afraid.'

'That's what concerns me.' He sighed. 'Go on, Fetherstone and the lads caught some turtles and they're making stew.'

'No giant lizards?' I had half-believed Isaac—only because he wasn't much given to jesting.

'Keep your eyes open, you might see some yet.'

I was about to reply when something clouted me from behind. I went sprawling and caught a mouthful of sand. The barrel of salt rolled away from me.

'Sorry,' grunted Sedlow. He had a small knot of men with him and they snickered as they passed. I stood, feet sliding back in the sand. Old Dad clamped a hand on my shoulder. He knew Sedlow better than most—as the two lead carpenters on the ship they were supposed to work together. Most of the time though, they were in conflict. Sedlow thought it was beneath him to work with a former slave.

'Careful, lad,' Old Dad warned as I clenched my fists. 'You don't want to start something you can't finish.'

I sat myself between Dobbin and Corner when we reached the campsite. There was already a good fire going and I helped myself to some fish stew. Fetherstone and Old Dad were arguing about the best way to cook a turtle, while poor Paddy Carter actually did the cooking. Harwood had the turtle shell and was beating out a rhythm on it while other crewmen shot him irritated glances. I grinned. Harwood drove the other lads wild, always talking and fidgeting. The only one who didn't seem to mind was Dobbin. The two acted like brothers, though they could scarcely have looked less alike. Harwood was fair and freckled, tall, rangy, whereas Dobbin was swarthy and slight. It was rare to see one without the other's company.

'Bonny.'

I tipped the last of the stew into my mouth and lowered my bowl to look at Calico. He was on his feet.

'Come back to the ship,' he said. 'We're going to have *words* about the way you left my damn cabin.'

I tossed my bowl aside and stood. 'I didn't *touch* your cabin.'

'Exactly.' He clamped a hand down on my shoulder and steered me ahead of him. 'Before you stepped off the *Kingston* I told you to take a holystone to the boards and bring those scrapes right down. Imagine my surprise when I go back in the cabin to find…' He trailed off as we drew out of the crew's earshot.

'What a performance,' I drawled. 'You could give up this life of crime and take to the stage.'

He grinned. 'Why would I? All the pretty women chase pirates.'

'Urgh.' I glanced over my shoulder several times as we went, ensuring we had no unexpected company. 'How was the *Kingston*? Looked like a sweet sail from where we were.'

Calico's face opened up, boyish for a moment. 'She was,' he agreed. 'I suppose you want me to thank you, for pushing us to take her.'

'That's not the only thing you ought to thank me for. We'd both be gallows-bait for now if not for me.' I caught a glimpse of his wry expression through the darkness. 'I'm just saying, Barnet has a big smoking hole in his bow right now and I'm the one who put it there. He might even sink.'

'Don't get too hopeful.' But he was laughing and as we walked down the beach he took my hand. 'I missed you.'

'Prove it.'

He swung to face me and pressed his lips against mine. He tasted of brandy and salt.

'That's nice,' I whispered, trying not to lose my thoughts to the wind. 'But not what I meant. Let me back on the *Kingston* with you when we take to sail again. If I have to look at Sedlow's ugly mug for another leg of the voyage I'll go mad.'

'Do you ever stop...' He sighed, searching for the word. 'Scheming?'

'I'm not scheming.' I unlaced his shirt. 'I'm thinking ahead.'

'I'm starting to feel you're a dangerous kind of woman.'

'Mhm. Good.' I laughed and caught his hands before they could wander. 'So?'

'What? Annie...'

'So, if I sail on the *Kingston* with you, you won't have to miss me.'

'Just...hold steady until we reach Cuba. Can you do that for me? Keep your head down, don't sink the ship, and try not to get yourself murdered.'

'You don't want me?' I stepped away from him and grinned as he threw up his hands in frustration. 'You don't want me. That's all right. I understand. Maybe I'll see if Isaac's lonesome, seeing as he and I will at least be on the same ship.'

Some of the humour slipped out of his voice. 'Fortunately for you, Isaac's not that way inclined.'

'Really?'

'Don't ask him about it. What Isaac does with his shore time is his own business and he won't thank you for sticking your nose into it.' His eyes locked with mine. 'Would you really go to someone else? Someone else on the crew?'

'Like who? Harwood? Sedlow? *Fetherstone?* Rest easy, Calico.' I leaned in and let my lips brush his jaw. 'I'm not going to sleep with anyone below the rank of captain.' *And you're the one who saved me.*

I tried to put that out of my mind. I didn't like being beholden to him.

'Good. I'm a jealous man.'

'Then hold onto me,' I said, catching his shirtfront and pulling him close. 'And mind you don't let me go.'

6
BARNET

Barnet paced the ship, cold rage prickling the length of his spine. The crew of the *Albion* worked through the night to make repairs on the ship. There was a hole at the bow where she'd taken on water; damage to the foremast. They had lost a killick and a good section of the railing. His beautiful ship, bested by a rag-tag group of pirates. Mutineers. Thieves.

The crew worked in small knots, drinking small beer and chewing tobacco. Barnet could feel their glancing eyes on him. He knew they were not used to taking a loss, and it had stung. Already he had been forced to have the bosun flog three of them for insolence. Commanding a crew was always a delicate balance of discipline and success, and Barnet could feel that balance sliding out of place.

The only way to set it right was to finish what they had started: he would see Calico Jack's crew hanged. There was no turning back now.

'Captain.'

Barnet looked over his shoulder. The cook was a squat man with a heavy face and pock-marked skin.

'Sir, we are running low on salt pork and hardtack.' He ran his tongue over his wind-cracked lips. 'And soon, beer.'

They should have stopped to resupply but Barnet had made the decision to push on without any further delays. They had enough supplies to get them from Jamaica to Cuba. Some people called 'Calico' Jack Rackham 'Jack of Cuba', and his ships seemed to be on a course for those waters. It was the logical place to start: pirates always had their favourite ports in which to go to ground. If they found nothing in Cuba they would go on to Rackham's old haunt in Nassau.

'Halve the rations,' he said. He saw concern cross the cook's face and ignored it. 'If the men cannot live slim for a few days until we reach Cuba, they are softer than I thought.'

'Yes sir.' The cook wavered, opened his mouth as if to voice an opinion, then turned and retreated to the galley.

That night as the crew gathered in the mess, Barnet heard the buzz of resentment. They took it out on the cabin boy, of course. The boy was standing now at the end of the line for the meal. He had been there a long time; other crewmen kept pushing their way in front of him. He did not protest, keeping his head down and his shoulders up by his ears. Barnet felt a twinge of pity for the boy. He was reminded of himself at that age, lost and lonesome, skinnier than he should have been. A memory rose unbidden in his mind. He stamped it out. The boy was not seriously harmed, and he would be a stronger sailor for it.

Still, Barnet noticed the new bruises blooming out along the boy's arms and cheeks.

Martin Read noticed as well.

The tall man had been sitting with a knot of sailors but now he unfolded and walked, stooped, across the mess. He was still holding his bowl in one hand. He planted a hand on the cabin boy's shoulders and steered him around to the front of the line. Barnet saw panic flash across the boy's face; he must have known the crew wouldn't be pleased.

'Give the boy a fair helping,' Barnet heard Read tell the cook. He clapped the cabin boy's shoulder and tipped the remains of his own meal into the lad's bowl. 'There.'

Angry stirrings from the other men waiting in line. Barnet shook his head. He understood the impulse but it would cause more trouble for the lad in the end. And for Read. The meal passed in a subdued lull but when the cabin boy stood to go about his duties, three other men finished their meals and climbed the companionway after him. Read, unhurried, scraped his plate and followed. He looked calm but as he climbed onto the deck Barnet saw him take a belaying pin from its place.

'Bosun.'

The boatswain, Hutch—Thomas Hutchinson—swallowed his mouthful and hastened to Barnet's side. 'Sir.'

'Let them rough the lads up a bit. Then halt the fight and punish them accordingly. No major damage, do you understand?'

'Sir.' The sound of fighting already clattered about the deck. Barnet did not approve of such displays but he hoped it would knock some sense into Read. There was a thud and the cabin boy yelped.

'Enough now, boys.' Hutch's voice rang out over the scuffle. Someone shouted. Barnet listened for Read's voice but could not make it out.

He straightened his jacket and went to the companionway, ready to survey the scene. He made his way briskly up the steps and pulled himself into the dying light of the day.

Two men were on the ground and a third was being hauled up by the bosun. They were bleeding and battered—one cradled his wrist against his chest. The cabin boy crouched between the mainmast and a barrel, one eye already swelling shut but otherwise unharmed.

And there stood Read. Straight-backed, ruffled but proud, his eyes blazing and his knuckles bloodied. Ignoring Barnet, he took a step towards the other three men. His voice was silken and low. 'I won't stand for cowards,' he said. 'Leave the boy alone.'

Barnet could have intervened but something stopped him. Perhaps he had misjudged something about Martin Read. He was not given to doubt, but for a moment he wavered, uncertain how to proceed.

'Enough.'

The men turned. Read was the last to face him, defiance tightening his features.

'I should have you flogged for such a display on my ship,' Barnet said. He studied them a moment more. Then he set his jaw. 'Get below. You're all on dog-watch until we reach Cuba. Move.' The men skirted past him. He caught Read's shoulder as the man went by. 'Not you.'

They waited until the other men went by. Barnet could feel Read's shoulder tense under his hand, ready to shrug him off.

'I must confess I am impressed, Read,' he said. 'I expected those men to beat you bloody.'

'I have seen war and worse,' Read said, and now he did shrug. Barnet removed his hand. 'I will not sit idle and watch grown men beat a youngster.'

Barnet nodded. 'You have some honour to you, Read,' he admitted, 'and you are a fine sailor. If you temper your insolence and accept command, you could do well on my crew. You might even find yourself an officer before too long.'

Read's features were blank. Carefully so, Barnet thought. Was he masking contempt or ambition? He pressed on.

'I want to see more from you, Read. You will have a chance to prove yourself when we apprehend John Rackham and his crew. Bear it in mind, and do not disappoint me.'

'Thank you, sir,' Read said at last. Barnet waited for more. More words, more gratitude, something other than that calm quiet across the tall man's face.

'Dismissed,' he said after a while, when he realised Read was done talking. Read nodded politely, turned on his heel and went below. Barnet was left on the deck, perplexed by the other man's attitude. As a young man, he would have been glad to have his captain's approval. He remembered volunteering for the dog-watch for weeks on end, just to make himself useful. Well, that and to catch the eye of...

He stopped himself. Thinking of her brought no joy, even after so many years. He refused to dwell on shadows of the past.

There was work to do.

7
BONNY

During months at sea, only catching slim moments of privacy, Calico and I had perfected the art of sneaking around. After a short time together on the dark beach, we righted our clothes, brushed the sand away from one another, and he went back to the crew and fire. I stayed as I was, knowing to wait a good hour more before I joined him. He would tell the crew he had left me to stew over it on the beach. I would collect palm fronds and other kindling for the fire and come back sullen and rebellious. Calico would ignore me for a day or so.

I drew patterns in the sand, lazy and comfortable. The nights were warm and peaceful. It was the dry season, so we didn't have to worry about hurricanes or wild storms, or the humid mugginess of the wet season. It was a blessed relief to be off the ship too, away from the stifling confines of the lower decks and the sun-baked swelter above. I knew we would only be on the island for a short while but it was enough to sit on solid ground.

I must have dozed for a short while. I found myself leaning against a tree with a crick in my neck; whatever time had passed I was probably due to head back to the camp. I didn't rush, stooping every few steps to gather palm fronds and old coconut husks. I kept to the fringe of the beach and enjoyed the cool push of the breeze.

'All alone, Bonny?'

In the space of a breath Sedlow had my shoulders and someone had my feet and I couldn't twist out of their grip. I struggled and craned. Sedlow's thick arm went about my neck. Someone's hold slipped, dropping me to the side. My face pressed into the crook of Sedlow's arm and I bit hard. He dropped me. One of the men still had my legs—my torso flopped down, sending a spasm of pain through my back. Sand in my mouth. They dragged me. I glanced off a rock and the world shook. Sedlow grunted and grabbed me under the arms.

They were taking me to the water.

The realisation paralysed me for a poisonous moment. Then I opened my mouth, filled my lungs to shriek. Sedlow's big hand clapped over my mouth.

I bucked and thrashed. We reached the waves and they slipped once more, this time letting my legs drop. I bent at the knees, tried to push up and back. One thought splintered in my mind: *They don't need deep water to drown me.*

Someone pushed me down. A heavy hand held the back of my neck and another twisted in my hair. I didn't have time to close my mouth. Saltwater rushed me, burning my eyes, my nose, my throat. They hauled me up as I spluttered and choked, then water engulfed me again. This time when they dragged me to the surface Sedlow leaned down to speak in my ear.

'No one here to step in this time. You showed me up, Bonny. It won't happen again.'

Even if I'd had the wit to answer, I didn't have the breath. My lungs ached. I tried to bring my hands up to loosen Sedlow's grip on me but one of his other cronies locked my arms behind my back. They ducked me again, pushing my face into the water. My nose hit the sand. Pain exploded in front of my eyes.

James stood in the doorway. He swayed like a man at sea, holding a jug in one hand. I drew away from the centre of the room and shrank into a corner. Lurching in, he slapped the jug down onto the table and dropped into a chair. His red-rimmed eyes found me in the gloom.

'I never should have married you,' he slurred. 'Nothing but bad luck since.'

All my life I'd been quick-tongued but I didn't dare run my mouth at him. I had nowhere else to go, no one to turn to.

'Come here,' he said.

I climbed to my feet. There was no point delaying the inevitable. He was a strong man and the streets of Nassau were deadly at night.

'Things will get better,' I said, treading soft across the dirt floor of the hut. 'We've only been here a few weeks. Give it time—'

He broke my nose.

And then, just like that, they let me go. I fell limp in the water. It took everything to push myself to my hands and knees. The waves battered me. I coughed and spat sand and blood into the water. Sedlow kicked me and I dropped again. They left me then, shaking and silent in the waves, gasping like a hooked fish. I couldn't hear the sea over the rasp and whistle of my own breath. Slowly, biting on pain, I crawled to dry sand and rolled onto my back.

The stars seemed to swim in a rippling sky. Slowly, feeling came back to my hands and feet. I breathed from my stomach and when I could, I went back to the water and washed the blood, snot and tears from my face. I took off my breast-bindings and focused on taking air into my abused lungs.

My limbs stopped shaking.

The wild panic faded, leaving a weather-smoothed stone of anger.

Most of the men had sauced themselves to sleep by the time I returned to the camp. They sprawled across the sand in their breeches, empty jugs nearby. Sedlow and his boys were on the other side of the camp. They watched me as I came in. Sedlow sat back, a smug smile hitched to his lips. He knew I wouldn't say anything to Calico. I was many things, but not a rat.

I looked to find my captain but he was asleep. Had he even noticed I was missing? Dawn would soon be upon us. Had he worried? Stared at the trees, waiting for my return? I set my jaw. Obviously not. But there'd be fewer questions this way.

I sank down at the base of a tree and pulled my bag over.

'Bonny.'

Spitting out a curse, I jumped to the side. It took me a moment to realise it was Isaac who had spoken. He sat with his back against a barrel. I had forgotten Isaac would be awake. The man's dreams were troubled.

We stared at one another. Then Isaac's eyes flicked in Sedlow's direction. Shame prickled through me. I knew what I must have looked like. Wet, bedraggled, bruised. Still bleeding from my nose, no matter how many times I swiped it away. Pathetic.

'Go back to sleep, Isaac,' I said, dropping onto my side and rolling over. Nothing was broken but everything hurt and I couldn't shake the ghost of fear. My stomach threatened to rebel. My mind was stuck behind me—not in the wild moments when I thought Sedlow would drown me, but in Nassau. In the wooden shack I had shared with James Bonny for those two dark years.

I wanted to go to Calico, to let him chase away the memories with his warmth and saltwater kisses. I wanted to scold him for not caring I was gone so long, and I wanted him to make it right. I wanted *him*.

And I couldn't help but think maybe that was a weakness in itself.

For the next two days Sedlow didn't spare me so much as a glance. That angered me more than anything. He knew he'd won.

My muscles were locked and sore, my bruises angry and swollen in the pale light of the morning. It was warm already but I pulled on my short-coat to cover my arms; I didn't want to wear the badge of my humiliation for everyone to see.

I avoided Calico and kept close to Old Dad as we careened the two ships. He and I had the task of fixing the heads of the *Ranger*, which we had pulled up onto the beach during high tide. There was loose planking and the lads had been complaining about it since Jamaica. As it was no one ever felt more vulnerable than when they were using the heads: a small hollowed box at the bow of the ship with a clear drop to the ocean below. On rough days the ocean could come right up through it, which had the advantage of washing your arse clean, but you couldn't say it was the most comfortable place to empty your bowels.

The smell there was foul. Collecting wood and shaping it on the beach was good work but hanging upside-down in a shit hole, prying out the old, stained planks, was more than my stomach could take. Dad tried to distract us both by talking about his old captain. He and Calico had both sailed under a man named Charles Vane but Calico had led a mutiny when Vane's courage failed and they lost a prize because of it. I delighted in these morsels of information about Calico's life before me. I felt like a naughty child, sneaking food that somehow tasted better for being stolen.

About halfway through, my stomach finally rebelled, and I had to shuffle away from the work and empty my belly into a bush. I kicked sand over it and waited for it to settle, then ate some hardtack and joined the others to help clear the camp.

Calico stamped out the remaining embers of the fire. I felt his eyes on me as I worked. I knew he wanted me to meet his gaze but I couldn't bring myself to do it. I'd been avoiding him since Sedlow and his boys jumped me. Flashes of the attack came at me now. *All alone, Bonny?* The sea and the sand. Pain and panic. I ground my teeth.

'I'm assigning you to the *Kingston* for the final leg to Cuba.' He spoke the words like a peace offering. I gathered the pans Paddy Carter had used for the dinner. 'You can swap with Carter.'

It was all I had wanted since we took the *Kingston* in the first place. But I took one glance at Sedlow and knew it would give him satisfaction.

I spoke low in case anyone was listening in. 'I'm fine where I am.'

Sedlow shouldered his way past Old Dad, made some comment to him. I didn't hear the words but I figured it was something unpleasant. Old Dad said nothing but his face settled into a taut smile.

'I want to stay on the *Ranger*,' I said.

Calico straightened and faced me. Confusion deepened the furrow between his brow. I wondered if he felt hurt. A small part of me hoped he did.

'You're sure?'

'I'm sure.'

The rest of the crew walked ahead of us, moving down to the beach. Calico took advantage of the onshore breeze, speaking quietly so no one else could hear.

'What happened the other night? You were gone a long time.'

'Don't you concern yourself, Jack.'

'*You're* concerning me.'

'I have things to take care of.'

He grabbed my arm. Old fear flashed through me and it was all I could do not to hit him. As it was I shrugged him off and took a step back.

'What is it?' he asked. 'What's changed?'

'Nothing's changed, captain.' I sharpened my voice, used it to fend him off. If Sedlow suspected anything lay between Calico and me, he'd turn it against us both. I had enough to worry about without that. For now, I would have to keep Calico at arm's length.

He opened his mouth to argue or appeal but one of the men called back to him, asking about watch schedules. He wavered, torn, then left me and joined the rest of the crew. I didn't see him again until we were both on our separate ships. Once the capstan was turned and the anchor was weighed I caught a glimpse of him, standing at the stern of the *Kingston* while they sailed ahead of us. I leaned on the railing. If I'd had any sort of heart at all I would have waved to him, blown a kiss, risked being found out in order to let him know all was well between us.

Instead I turned away and went below.

8
BONNY

The men on the ship knew me as a cocky little bastard but I had no illusions about my size or strength. I had a good eye and good balance, and I was nimble. I could hold my own with Dobbin and Harwood. It didn't mean much against men twice my weight, with a good head and shoulders on me. Men who had me outnumbered.

I took stock of the crew on the *Ranger*: Dobbin and Harwood, Corner, Isaac, Sedlow, a small knot of Sedlow's boys and myself. I didn't like those odds. Sedlow and his boys were obviously a danger to me. Dobbin and Harwood would be too busy larking about and pissing off the side of the ship to be much help. Corner was a decent fellow but he was the quartermaster and couldn't be seen to take sides in crew disputes. That left me with Isaac. He'd stepped between me and Sedlow before, but he also liked to keep his hands clean. And I knew better than to presume his friendship with Calico extended as far as me.

If I had been too hasty in refusing Calico's offer, I didn't let the thought cloud my mind for long. I needed to take Sedlow to task.

And after all, there were a thousand ways a man could die at sea.

I waited until Sedlow and his boys were drunk. We weren't supposed to indulge in hard drink at sea but Calico was on the other ship. The seas were good, Isaac was on the helm, and there was no sight of Jonathan Barnet and the *Albion*. The lads didn't need much encouragement to take to the brew. Only Isaac stayed on his task. He said he wasn't in the mood to drink and dice, but I had a feeling he was trying to avoid Sedlow's crowd. I sympathised.

I made do with small beer—watered down until it wasn't much more than a tickle on my tongue. I played it up though, letting my voice get loud and brash. Dobbin and Harwood drank against one another, getting stupider as the evening grew. Harwood got loud when he was drunk and Dobbin got competitive. Sedlow was just as bad and I thanked God briefly for his arrogance.

As far as he was concerned I had been put in my place. He didn't have to worry about me anymore.

Corner put a stop to the drinking when Isaac sounded eight bells for midnight, prompting a loud chorus of complaints. The lads didn't have much fight in them, though, and one by one they made their way to the orlop to sleep, or to the open deck to sprawl themselves across the boards. One or two others stumbled to the heads, the combination of rough fare and rougher grog enough to upset their stomachs one way or another. Sedlow wouldn't be long, I was pretty sure. Before the drinking started I'd smeared his mug with rat-rotted bilge water.

Now I crouched in the shadow of the wooden barrier built around the heads. It didn't give much by way of privacy but I was small enough to make myself unseen in the cover of night. I waited, thighs burning. Eyes burning too, from the smell. It didn't matter. I could wait there all night if I had to, hoping Sedlow's mug-lining would loosen his bowels.

I'd almost given up hope when Sedlow lurched into the heads, shoving poor Dobbin out. Still struggling to drag up his breeches, Dobbin threw half-hearted curses in the big man's direction and stumbled away. I listened for the creak of the boards. Heard a quiet grunt.

I leaned forward and grabbed hold of the stick Old Dad and I had placed so carefully. Then I pushed.

There was a clack of boards, a grunt, a splash and a muffled shout. I flung myself into the heads. Sedlow was ale-addled, but not so far gone that he had been caught completely unawares. When the supporting planks had dropped into the water he'd managed to catch hold of the deck to save himself. He was dangling there now, above the open water, gripping the remaining wooden boards tightly. I couldn't see the ocean clearly, just a sucking, swallowing black. But I could hear it. The sea was hungry.

Sedlow's eyes widened when he saw me.

'Irish bastard!' he choked. His hands danced on the wood, trying to get a better grip. His breeches were still around his ankles. 'Let me up!'

I usually went barefoot at sea but tonight was different.

His fingers crunched beneath my boots.

Sedlow howled but the noise cut off when I kicked him in the face: his head snapped backwards and the rest of him followed. I watched him as he dropped. The sea took him whole and the *Ranger* ploughed over him.

I stood there, staring at the black waters, waiting until my breath came back to me. Then I shrank out of the heads and climbed over the wooden structure to where Old Dad and I had hidden the replacement. It didn't take a lot of time or effort to simply slot it into the place where the other heads had been. I tested it carefully to be sure no one else would fall through. Then I strolled out of the heads and made my way across the deck.

'I saw that.'

'Isaac,' I hissed. 'God rot your eyes, I almost shat myself! Stop *doing* that!'

'I saw that,' he repeated. His hands were firm on the wheel, his eyes firm on me.

'Saw what?'

'Was that your idea? Or Dad's?'

No point pretending. 'My idea. Dad's handiwork.'

'You know the penalty for murder?'

I tensed. Isaac was a big man, and a careful one. And Calico's best friend. Would he tell? What sort of choice would Calico be left with? Only to maroon me, or execute me outright.

'I know.' My mouth was dry, my mind flitting through different options. I didn't think I'd be able to bribe Isaac. I couldn't threaten him. According to Jack I wouldn't even be able to seduce him.

'Well.' We stood facing one another for a short while, only the waves and wind murmuring between us. Then Isaac seemed to arrive at a decision. His grip on the helm relaxed. 'Shame about Sedlow. I warned him he was leaning too far over.'

Relief made me weak at the knees. 'Never a good listener.'

Isaac's face lifted and for a moment he looked like he would smile. Then he twisted it into a glare.

'Go below, Bonny,' he said. 'Keep your head down.'

Richard Corner called me into the captain's cabin the next morning. It was strange, being in Calico's cabin without him. Half his possessions were still there.

'Isaac said you saw Sedlow go overboard.'

I shrugged. 'Aye.'

'What happened?'

'Sedlow went overboard.'

Corner's heavy face dropped into a glower. 'Don't give me any of your cheek, boy,' he growled. 'I'm the one who has to report this to the captain. *What happened?*'

I didn't hesitate. 'Sedlow was pissing over the side and he thought he saw something in the water. He leaned out. Isaac told him to mind. Sedlow said something about not taking orders from a slave, and then he lost his balance and over he went.' Isaac and I had conferred about the details before dawn fell.

'Where was he?'

'Starboard, near the bow.'

'Where were you?'

'Talking to Isaac.'

'And neither of you helped him once he was over? Tried to throw down a rope?'

'We were going at quite a clip last night.' I shrugged.

'Anyway, Sedlow was a real bastard to Isaac and Old Dad. Didn't much like me either.'

'And?'

'And neither of us, Isaac or me, wanted to risk our arses for someone who would just as happily drop us over the side.' I folded my arms. 'So no. I can't speak for Isaac but if you want the honest truth from me I don't care about Sedlow as much as I would *any* drowned bilge-rat.'

Corner sat back in Jack's chair, staring at me. 'Think you're a hard lad, don't you, Bonny?'

'You asked.'

'How old are you?'

'Fourteen.' I paused. 'Thereabouts.' I was eighteen in truth, but it was easier for me to pass as a boy than a young man.

Corner scratched his beard. 'Can I give you some advice?'

'I imagine you probably will.'

'Bonny, you're smart as a whip. You're a good shot, you climb like a monkey and it's no secret you make the captain laugh as much as you make him hopping mad. You'll make a damn fine sailor if you *just keep quiet long enough to live out a year*.' He put a big hand on my shoulder. 'I'm happy to believe you and Isaac. You were in the wrong place at the wrong time last night. But from now onwards, you make it your business to be in the right place at the right time. Understand?'

A hundred responses went through my head but I knew only one would end the conversation. 'Yes, sir.'

'Go on, then.'

I sauntered out of the cabin, grinning at Isaac as I passed him by. He frowned, making a clear point: our brief alliance was not a friendship. I went on past him without a second look, telling myself I didn't care. But a small part of me was disappointed. Without Calico or Old Dad on board, I felt alone.

Still, it would only be a few days before we reached Cuba.

9

BONNY

Next morning was the first time I realised something was wrong. I'd always found it uncomfortable to bind my chest but now it *hurt*. I crouched in the orlop, frantically trying to work through the pain before any of the lads came back down. That done, I fumbled with the lacing on my breeches. Had they always been this tight?

That wasn't all, though.

Until Nassau my monthly courses had come and gone regular as the moon itself. Now I tried to figure how long it had been since my last bleed. Too long. Two months at least. I'd been so preoccupied with learning the ways of the ship and crew, with keeping my secrets, with Sedlow, that I hadn't given it much thought. I'd just been relieved not to deal with it.

Other details started to click into place: my 'battle-shakes'; how lonely and miserable I'd felt in the last few days; how badly my back ached after Sedlow and his boys ducked me in the ocean, even when my other hurts had faded.

My mother died when I was thirteen. I'd not had her to teach me about the ways of men and women, but I'd spent a lot of time in my father's kitchen, listening to the slaves and servants talk. I'd watched when one of the slaves about my age, a girl named Phibe, grew swollen and sore with child. She had worked—hard field work—right up until the day of her labour. Then her screams had echoed through the quiet corners of the plantation. Neither she nor her child survived a day.

How could I have been so thick? How did I not realise?

'Bonny?' Dobbin stuck his head down the companionway. 'You gonna sleep all day? Come on, we'll make Isla de Pinos by noon.'

I tried to collect my scattered thoughts. 'Isle of Pines?'

'Isle of Pines,' he confirmed.

'Why are we stopping short of Cuba?'

'We want to avoid Havana if we can,' he clarified. 'Captain's too well-known there.'

I didn't know much about Calico's childhood. I knew he'd spent a lot of it in Cuba, that he had friends there; he never said more. I tried to imagine him as a boy. He would have been errant and reckless, dragging himself and others into scrapes and even outright danger. It felt strangely like a loss, to be so excluded from his childhood. All the details I had of him came from the other men, and they were sparse enough as well.

It was one of the many things that teetered in balance between us, unspoken.

How are we going to discuss this, *Calico?*

I could thank God in his questionable mercy that I'd never had a child to James Bonny. But what would Calico do? Would he find me some apothecary's tonic to kill it in the womb? Kick me off the ship and leave me on the shore as a kept woman? Could I expose myself as a woman to the crew and raise a brat on a pirate ship? Grace O'Malley was said to have done so...

The last thought was so stupid it took my breath away. This was no Irish ballad. Women were called the Devil's ballast—bad luck on any voyage. If the men found out they would kill me; that, or lock me in the brig and take turns with me, and Calico might not even stop them. These men were pirates, for God's sake. I was under no illusions about them. The moment they knew I was a woman they would become a mortal danger to me.

'Oh, Calico,' I said under my breath.

'What?' Dobbin looked over his shoulder at me.

'Nothing.' I climbed the companionway into the bright light of the morning.

Old Dad was the first person I saw when we reached land. He came up to help us beach the jolly-boat and I saw his dark eyes flick over the rest of the skeleton crew, searching for Sedlow. Then he looked back at me and his crooked teeth flashed into a warm grin. My heart wasn't in the smile I gave back. Sedlow's death was not a comfort to me, not at this moment.

Once the boat was secured we walked along the beach. Old Dad drove a bony elbow into my ribs.

'Well?'

'Worked beautifully,' I admitted.

'Anyone see you?'

'Isaac. We came to an understanding on the matter.'

Old Dad nodded. 'Isaac's a decent man. Knows how to hold his tongue. Corner ask you any questions?'

'Just the ones he had to. We're clear.'

'Good lad.' His eyes narrowed on me in the silence that followed. 'Don't take it hard, boy. Men like Sedlow, it's always you or them eventually. Killing gets easy once you realise that.'

A small part of me knew that killing shouldn't be easy. I should have been more concerned with the guilt than with the quickening child in my belly. But I'd signed on for piracy, and here we were. Sedlow had been washed away with the filth from the heads. He wasn't my problem anymore.

'It doesn't bother me,' I said truthfully. 'Where's the captain?'

Old Dad rolled his eyes. 'Fetherstone and Paddy Carter are about ten paces away from a duel,' he said. 'Captain's trying to level it out before Paddy shoots George in the face.'

So Jack would be irritated and fretful before I even told him anything. And he hadn't heard about Sedlow yet.

'Thanks for your help with Sedlow,' I said to Old Dad as we walked up the beach. It sounded grudging but I was being sincere.

He snorted. 'Sedlow's been giving me French gout for the better part of a year now. I think about the *Ranger* ploughing over him and it's like a lullaby. Especially when you add the fact that he fell to his death with his breeches around his ankles.'

'God's eyes, Dad, keep your voice down!'

He grinned. 'Go on, find something to eat before you find the captain. You know he's bound to have some reason to send you back to the ship on scrubbing duties.'

He didn't know the half of it.

I found Calico on the shore. He was frazzled, his hair standing on end from where his hands had raked it in frustration. It wasn't an easy job, keeping our crew in line. I wasn't anywhere near the only troublemaker.

I didn't want to bring him ill news, not when he was already wild-eyed, but I knew if I didn't tell him now I never would. My hand itched to slip into his. Instead I buried both of them deep in my pockets and slouched my shoulders.

'We have a problem.'

'I know,' he snapped. '*Bloody* Paddy Carter.'

'That's not what I mean.'

'Say what you mean then, Bonny.'

I knew he was just being careful, not wanting to be heard even if we were some distance from the rest of the crew, but his tone rubbed away the sympathy I had felt for him.

'I'm in the family way, Jack.'

He stopped. Faced me properly. Pale to the lips. Seeing him afraid, the man who swung into battle in a calico coat, made me twitchy and nervous.

'I don't understand.' His voice, usually warm and strong, was flat.

Irritation flicked through me. 'Yes you do. I'm lugging your brat around in my belly.'

'What do we do?'

'You're the captain. You tell me.'

'Stop playing the clown!'

'Stop *raising your voice*.' We stood a short distance

from the crew, on the pretext of discussing Sedlow's death. The only good thing about this baby so far was that it saved me from *that* particular conversation. I took a deep breath and went on more calmly. It was somehow easier to be level when he was panicking. 'I'm not worried, Calico. I can manage this all myself, and I will. But I thought you at least deserved to know. We're going to have to come up with some excuse for me to leave the ship, and then I'll have to find a place to stay on land until the thing is born. Once that's done with, I'll meet up with you and we can go along as if nothing happened.'

'You don't want to keep it?'

'What would we do with a baby, Calico?'

He just shook his head.

For a moment I felt sorry for him again. 'Would you let me keep it on the ship?' I prompted.

'No.'

'Would you stay on land with me to raise it?'

'No.' No hesitation there. Calico had stolen the position of captain and he intended to keep it.

'Then there's nothing more to be said on the matter. I'll be damned if I'm going to stay on land and keep house for you while you sail around the world having adventures. No. If you're at sea, I'm at sea.'

'And the child?'

'I'll think of something.'

'You may not be able to just "think of something",
Annie.'

I managed a smile. 'Ridiculous man.' I turned back
towards the camp and he caught my arm.

'Annie.'

'What?'

'Do you love me?'

I almost thought I could feel the babe squirming, but
it was too early for that. It was just Calico's earnestness.

'Ah, Calico.' I pulled my hand away and rubbed the
back of my neck. 'I came to sea with you, didn't I?'

I couldn't watch his disappointment. Neither could
I tell him what he wanted to hear. I'd been in love, and it
was a short road to a long heartache.

'Anyway,' I said, trying to lighten my voice. 'If you
have any friends in Cuba who might want a baby, now is
the time to send a message.'

He didn't say anything for a while. When he spoke
again, his voice was subdued. 'I know a couple. Walter
and Rose Cunningham. You can stay with them. They've
wanted children for years and had none.'

'Good.' I felt the knots easing out of my shoulders.
Calico's eyes were on the sea. Usually they were a bright
clear blue, but now they seemed closer to grey. He stood
very straight. There was colour high in his cheeks. I felt
guilty for shrugging him off, and resentful about it. More
than anything I wanted to slip my arms around him

and make him smile. To quench the strange hollowness that had been growing in me since we left the last island. I reached for his elbow.

'Calico?'

He didn't look around. I withdrew my hand and hesitated.

I would probably have gone to kiss him if Dobbin hadn't come around the beach at that moment. I stepped away from Calico and shoved my hands into my pockets, sinking my heels back into the sand, and glared at Dobbin. There was never a moment of peace with this crew. Someone always seemed to step in at exactly the wrong time.

'Captain, Paddy Carter says he's quitting,' Dobbin said.

'Tell Paddy I'll happily knock that idea out of his head,' Calico replied. He sighed and turned away from the sea. 'He can stand watch on the *Kingston* tonight.'

Dobbin's face eased. 'I'll tell him, captain.'

'You too, Bonny.'

I glanced at Calico, confused. His eyes barely flicked in my direction.

'Stay on the *Kingston* tonight,' he clarified. 'We need a few watching the vessels.'

'Yes, captain.' If I sounded sharp, he didn't react. I looked for warmth in his eyes and only found the clouds of a spent storm. His silence told me I was dismissed.

10
BARNET

Barnet hadn't intended to take the *Albion* to the islands surrounding Cuba but she was gathering weed and barnacles on her hull and the drag was compounding the problems wrought by the hasty repairs to the bow. The wind was good and the waters were clear, but the *Albion* moved through the waves like they were mud. The men were tired from patching leaks and constant pumping—and the stores had taken damage as well, leaving them with shortened rations. It made the crew sloppy and quarrelsome. Barnet spent as much time settling disputes as he did managing the damage to the ship.

The inconvenience rankled with him. He was not a patient man.

He strode across the quarterdeck as the sun crept out from the skin of the sea. At the companionway, he ducked his head to climb to the lower decks. The air was foul here, stale and thick. The men were at idle, dipping hardtack into their small beer, chewing on strips of dry meat. Some ruminated, like cattle, on tobacco. Smoking was forbidden.

The men started when they saw him, caught shirking. Some tried to step back into the shadows of the orlop, hoping not to be seen. Barnet made a note of each.

'Go to your duties,' he said, keeping his voice level. 'We drop anchor at the Isle of Pines for tonight.' It was a concession, an unspoken promise that the men would be permitted to leave the ship, to drink and stretch their land legs on the island for a few hours at least. He did not intend to stop long in Cuba, so this would soften that particular blow and appease them.

They scattered about their various tasks with renewed energy, talking in low voices. Casting an eye about the crewmen who moved past him, Barnet realised Martin Read was not among them. He narrowed his eyes and climbed the companionway. Was the man lounging somewhere? Indolent sailors could always find nooks and crannies in which to hide. Barnet had once found the cabin boy asleep beneath a coil of rope. The boy had been soundly whipped and had not tried such a thing since. Read was probably too tall for that trick but Barnet knew it was unwise to make assumptions. Particularly, he thought, about Martin Read.

He could not say, exactly, why the man bothered him so much. Perhaps it was his calm humour, which always seemed to be at Barnet's expense.

'Captain.'

Or perhaps it was the man's uncanny knack of knowing his mind.

Barnet stopped and clasped his hands behind his back. Read faced him, eyes gleaming and posture tense. The tall man was as slow to smile as Barnet himself but now a grin crept into his features.

Barnet frowned. 'Yes?'

'There is something you should see on the starboard side, sir.'

Barnet followed him back above deck, stopping only when he saw the sails protruding from the bay of the Isle of Pines. He leaned on the rail.

Floating in the bay was a neat little craft, a merchant sloop. She was next to new, her sails still pale and her lines clean and fine. The work of a talented shipwright. And from her mast, fanning out in the light breeze that blew in off the water, was a black flag. A skull over two crossed swords.

Barnet's heart quickened. The ache in his temples, present since the failed hunt, slipped away.

'I know this ship,' he murmured. 'I know that flag.'

Entirely by accident, they had stumbled on Calico Jack and his stolen prize.

A quiet thrill went through Barnet. Of all the islands, all the bays, all the places the pirates could have stopped…

As if God had delivered them into his hands.

11
BONNY

Noah Harwood and I were having a spitting contest. He had me for distance but no one could match my aim. It was a stupid way to spend the afternoon but it distracted me from thinking about the chill in Calico's voice when he'd sent me over to the *Kingston*. Distracted me from the sick feeling in my belly, the constant reminder that something was alive and growing in there.

The *Ranger* was tucked into another bay on the island. Isaac had argued we were too much of a target with two visible ships. Calico, knowing we were safe out here, had looked exasperated, but Isaac had eventually persuaded him to be cautious. A couple of the other lads were on the *Ranger* and a few of us were posted to the *Kingston*. With good weather, flat seas and not another ship in sight, there wasn't much else to do but pass the pale morning spitting.

'You're both idiots.' Isaac passed us by with a wooden bowl in one hand.

'Jealous,' I shot back. Harwood hawked and spat out at the ocean. I handed him a jug of small beer, laughing. 'Nice.'

Harwood swigged from the jug. 'So what'd you do?' he asked, wiping his mouth.

'What do you mean?'

'Isaac wanted to stay back. Paddy Carter's here because he and Fetherstone keep trying to kill one another. Ashcroft is here because he tried to smuggle a pipe below decks. Dobbin and me, we volunteered because Dobbin stowed a barrel of gin and the others don't know about it. But everyone knows you make the captain madder'n a stuck pig and that you get too restless to keep onboard of your own offering. So what did you do to get sent back this time?'

I sighed and took the jug from him. 'Said something stupid,' I shrugged. 'For a change…'

I trailed off, catching sight of movement off our port beam. I shoved the jug back into Harwood's hands and scrambled to my feet. 'Isaac, are you seeing this?'

He didn't answer, already below to find a spyglass. I grabbed a ratline to pull myself into the rigging for a better vantage point and my stomach dropped. I didn't need a spyglass to recognise the ship limping up on our stern.

The *Albion*.

I froze. Too late to run and we didn't have the crew to fight. The others were all on the island. Plenty of weapons—no one to wield them.

A heavy footfall sounded behind me. Isaac. He hadn't gone below to get a spyglass, as I'd thought, but had instead brought back an armful of firearms. I dropped down to the deck and took a flintlock for myself.

'We're going to lose the *Kingston*,' Isaac said. I choked on the idea. Harwood caught his breath. By this point Paddy and Dobbin were on the deck with us. They were both pale. Only Isaac was steady, calm. 'We don't have any options,' he went on. 'We load up a jolly and row like the Devil back to shore. We'll lose the prize but we still have our own ship. We won't lose more than we can afford.'

'Tell that to Calico,' I murmured, but the sound was lost under the thunder of cannon. The shot fell short. We jerked into motion, running to winch the jolly over the water. Isaac and Paddy, the strongest of us, stayed on the deck while Ashcroft, Dobbin and Harwood clambered from the railing into the small boat. I handed the boys our weapons and a few barrels of food, then dropped a rope ladder over the side and followed them, stepping over the railing into the boat. Once we were lowered into the water, Isaac and Paddy used the rope ladder to climb down.

The *Albion* was low at the bow but she moved fast enough. She came abreast of the *Kingston* on our starboard side. I thought she would stop there, but as we rowed towards the shore I saw her damaged bow re-emerging from the other side of the stolen ship. I realised in that moment it was not just about the prize, not for Barnet. He was coming for us, too.

I could see him at the bow: no mistaking him. Just as Calico wore his fine coat to battle, so it seemed did Barnet. He could have been mistaken for a military man, with the figure he cut. I poured powder into my flintlock, wadded and rammed it, then fitted my shot into the barrel. He had me for distance but no one could match my aim. I stood, struggling to balance as the small jolly turned on a sharp wave, and climbed over barrels and crates to stand at the prow.

'What are you doing?' Dobbin asked, his voice strangled. His rowing faltered until Harwood dug him in the side with his elbow.

'Steady, Bonny,' Isaac grunted.

I planted my feet. Levelled my gun. The *Albion* was coming about, preparing to cut us off from shore. I kept my eye on Barnet. Breathed out long and steady.

Then I fired. The flintlock jerked back in my hand. A scalding crack sounded.

Barnet was down and for a moment I thought I'd hit him. A surge of elation ran through me, followed by the sharp drop of disappointment. Someone had pushed Barnet down. I saw both men rise, unscathed.

I muttered a curse and fumbled to clean the barrel of my flintlock so I could reload. Seconds later a gun roared and the shot dropped close: water shattered across the small jolly-boat. Barnet ran along the deck and then I couldn't see him anymore.

'The helmsman,' Isaac said. 'Fire on the helmsman! Don't let anyone take the—'

I didn't give him a chance to finish the sentence. My gun was reloaded. I whirled, steadied, aimed, and shot the helmsman on the *Albion*. He slumped forward onto the wheel. Ashcroft fed me more ammunition as I readied the flintlock a third time. If no one could take the helm, it would give us the chance we needed.

Dobbin and Harwood took over the oars and Isaac came to crouch at my shoulder. He had a good eye as well, and a double-barrelled musket. If I'd been blessed with longer arms I would have preferred the weapon myself—it was a dream for accuracy. Isaac and I maintained the pressure on the helm. The *Albion* lurched, lost without someone to guide her. Triumph fluttered in my stomach as we pulled away from the ship.

And then the world exploded into splinters and heat.

All I knew was water and pain.

My lungs screamed. I couldn't see. I kicked but couldn't find the surface. The chest-bindings restricted my movement and my breath. My cheek hurt, my legs, one of my arms. I rolled in the water and tried to swim but there was no direction, no *light*. Panic strangled the remaining air out of my chest.

And then I was pulled sidewards. I broke the water, gasped and choked and realised I'd been swimming down. Saltwater poured out of my mouth. Strong arms hauled me clear and wrapped me, pinning my arms to my side. I knew I was hurt, knew I was bleeding. Spots danced and grew in front of my eyes. The air came too quickly into my lungs and I couldn't take it evenly. I clamped my mouth shut and forced myself to slow down. I couldn't stop shaking.

I wondered about the baby in my belly. If it was even still alive.

'Took your damn sweet Godforsaken time, Isaac!' I finally managed to rasp, jerking out of my frozen, spluttering quiet. The salt made my voice rough.

'I am not Isaac.'

The unfamiliar voice brought the panic back. I tried to struggle but I was still wheezing for air and when I moved my arm it felt like it was being torn off.

His grip tightened. 'Be still, little fellow. No need for anyone to get hurt.'

'I killed one of you bastards already, I'll gladly kill more!'

'No need for anyone *else* to get hurt,' he conceded. He stood, dragging me. I couldn't put weight on my right leg. I didn't bother checking if my guns had survived; the water would have ruined the powder. I craned my neck to get my bearings. I was on a jolly-boat. In the shadow of a ship, presumably the *Albion.* There were maybe seven other men in the boat and one of them had a gun trained on me.

In the distance, I saw Isaac and the others pulling our own half-splintered jolly towards the shore. They left it there and ran up the beach in a hail of fire from the *Albion.* A flash of anger burned hot in my throat. They hadn't hesitated long before leaving me behind.

'You're going to make a sensible decision now.' The man holding me had a pale, quiet voice with a strange accent. English? Flemish? 'If you fight, we will shoot you. But if you come gently to the ship, and do as the captain commands, you may find us lenient.'

Take your leniency and be damned. The words didn't make it past my lips. Lack of strength or lack of courage? I slumped in the man's grip. I prayed the babe would hold tight: if I started bleeding now they would find me out as a woman and God only knew what they would do.

The man who held me was strong. As tall as Isaac, but not quite as solid. He carried me onto the ship on his back; there was no chance I could make the climb on my own. I hadn't had a chance to take stock of my injuries but now the desperate fight for survival was over, I was starting to feel them.

He didn't drop me onto the deck. I almost wished he had, just so I could lie down and curl around my sore ribs. Instead, he eased me from his back and turned me so one of the other men could bind my hands. My arm was bleeding, probably cut by the jagged wood of the damaged jolly-boat as I fell out of it. My ribs didn't feel cracked but they were bruised. My knee was swelling and ugly. Nothing seemed broken but I was battered and wheezing and my crewmates had left me behind.

Were they relieved to be rid of me at last?

The crew surrounding me was not of the navy, but they dressed smarter than most of the sailors I'd met. They jostled and shuffled forward, making a rough half-ring around me. Death in their eyes. I could see their fallen comrade set out on the deck, wrapped in canvas. The remaining men were angry, and they had good reason for it. My mind strayed towards thoughts of the noose, the gibbet. I fought back a shudder.

No weakness, no cowardice. I stood crooked on my bad leg but I forced myself to rights and straightened my shoulders.

'Pirate.'

Someone spat on me. It opened a door. A murmur sprang up among the other men, a slow press forward. Maybe I didn't have to worry about the noose or the baby at all. Maybe I was going to die right here and now.

'Stop.' The man who held me was soft-spoken but his one word was enough to halt the other sailors. 'He sees the captain first.'

My bravado faltered when he shepherded me forward. My knee buckled with every step. Still, I noticed the other men stepped clear to let us through. To let *him* through. I found myself wondering what he had done to gain such respect—or fear. Perhaps I'd never find out.

Barnet's cabin was well-lit and spacious. A small table was nailed to the boards, detailed charts stretched across it. There was a cot in the corner, neat and plain. No playing cards or dice strewn across the floor, no clothes dropped carelessly or draped over the cot. No books, which I might have expected from an educated man, and no portraits or trinkets. At the end of the cot was a trunk, which probably contained clothing, and a pair of boots. I couldn't smell drink or tobacco. It was all clean, sparse.

And then there was Barnet himself.

You would never know the man had just captured a ship, regardless of how paltry our resistance had been. You wouldn't even guess he was *on* a ship, just by looking at him. He was smartly groomed, his clothes simple and neat, close to military in style. There was something stiff and old-fashioned about him. He was not an old man, though. Just a man of the old world.

'Read.' He nodded and the man behind me released my arms and stepped away. Then Barnet took a pace forward. He wasn't tall, but like most men he was taller than me.

'What is your name, boy?'

'Ned Fletcher.' My father's clerk in Charles Town: a young, skinny, serious boy who had left us for England the year before I married James Bonny. It was the most distant name I could think of.

'You are going to hang for your crimes, Ned Fletcher.' He clasped his hands behind his back. 'We will transport you back to Port Royal, where you will be imprisoned and trialled. Once you are found guilty—*and you will be*—you will hang from the neck until dead. Your corpse will be tarred and strung up in a gibbet.'

'Sounds like a busy day.'

He hit me in the face, an open-handed blow. I felt the impact before I felt the pain. My head snapped back. Read caught me and held me fast.

I spat onto the deck and forced air into my constricted lungs.

'May God have mercy on your soul,' Barnet said, as if he fancied himself a priest now. He rubbed his hand absently. 'Read, take him below.'

Read took my arms again and steered me away from Barnet. He didn't say a word, and I wouldn't have heard if he had. My mind was churning, trying endless avenues of escape that all seemed to end with death. The crew bundled close to us. They watched me go, hatred on their faces.

The brig was small and musty. Read didn't push me in but he was careful to lock the door behind me. I turned to look through the bars at him. He was lean and broad-shouldered, with dark hair and clear eyes. They were fixed on me now.

There was nothing to sit on so I used the inside wall of the brig to ease myself down to the deck. My knee gave out beneath me and I sat splay-legged. I knuckled my forehead, trying to ease the nausea that was roiling my gut.

I didn't doubt they would question me. I was afraid of my own fear; of weakness. I feared telling Barnet each and every one of Calico's secrets, spilling the waters of the whole crew for the sake of my own skin. No one lasted long during torture. A man would tell everything he knew, say whatever he was told to say, just to make it stop.

I didn't look at Read. Should I come clean? They couldn't hang me if I was with child. Would they take me to Carolina, back to my father? Or would they drag me to my husband in Nassau? Both were a kind of death. My father would have my marriage annulled and bind me to one of his wealthy friends, twice my age. I would have children and die sweating and trapped in the Charles Town humidity. My husband...

James' eyes were bloodshot. Drink made him clumsy but it also made him cruel. I crouched in a corner and nursed my swollen jaw. I hated how timid he had made me. Each moment with him, I watched carefully for signs he was going to hurt me.

'I am speaking to you, little fellow.'

I stared at Read. Banished the memory. Whatever happened to me from now, I would not go back to James Bonny.

'I will send for some cloth,' Read said at last. Conversational, calm, as if he had not just imprisoned me. 'You need to strap that knee.'

Once I had strapped my leg Read and I exchanged no words for some hours. My tongue, usually so quick to insult or curse, felt numb and dry in my mouth. I was tired, and thoughts of my husband were never far away.

On several occasions, crewmen came down to the brig. Armed. Muttering. But they stopped when they saw Read and after a few tense moments they always retreated. I didn't blame them. A few hours in I noticed he'd found himself a marlinespike and it rested across his knees. Whether he had it to deter them from brutality or me from escape I didn't know, but it was effective on both counts.

At some point one of the other lads brought across something for Read to eat, as well as a strong drink. He offered some to me when we were alone. I drank: I could be proud but I wasn't stupid. The alcohol numbed some of the throbbing pain in my knee and arm, and around midday I finally managed some sleep. It was cramped and uncomfortable and I awoke with a stiff neck, but I felt more myself.

'You're small for a pirate.' It was the first thing Read had said to me since he had brought cloth for me to strap my knee.

I shrugged. 'I run for the gunners,' I said. 'Powder-monkeys like me only work if they're small.'

'You're young for a pirate, too.'

But older than I looked. 'Oh, you know.' I tried to sound casual. 'Can't let the old men have all the fun.' My voice was light but I was wary. I didn't know how to figure Read. 'Why the marlinespike?' I was afraid to ask but I forced the words out of my mouth before I had too long to think about them.

He tapped it lightly on his knee. 'You killed one of our own.'

My fingers were cold and numb. I rubbed my hands to keep warm. My knee pulsed out a steady reminder of the jolly-boat splintering and cracking apart. 'And?'

'And the captain wants you delivered to Port Royal alive. The marlinespike is to remind the men.'

'Why does he care? I'll die either way.'

Read's lips curved. 'Captain Barnet likes things to be done in the proper fashion,' he said. 'If you are to die, you will die by the law. He will not have his men made murderers.'

'And he trusts you not to kill me?'

Read shrugged. 'The captain knows I have a hatred of cowards,' he said. 'I would not kill a skinny boy with a bad leg. If your leg was healed and you had more meat to your bones, I would untie you and face you on the beach with pistols.'

I forced a laugh. 'You would lose.'

'Why?'

'I'm a damn good shot. You've seen that.'

He looked amused. 'You are an arrogant little fellow, aren't you?'

'I have reason to be.' I shuffled my shoulders against the wood at my back, trying to get comfortable. I was playing for time, trying to work out what sort of a man Read was. Soon enough I'd need to piss. Fine if I could use the heads but I suspected I wouldn't be given the privilege. There was a bucket in the corner and sooner or later I'd have to drop my trousers and go there. I had a feeling *that* particular situation would raise some questions. I doubted I would have much privacy even when we reached Cuba.

I didn't want to tell Read what I was. That was too much knowledge for a man to hold over my head. Decent as he seemed, all that separated any man from evil was opportunity and stiff nerves. That even applied to Calico, I told myself, though he had never hurt me. He'd had every opportunity and instead he'd…

I couldn't deliberate forever. Could I seduce Read? Perhaps. I figured a sailor would be an easy mark, alone at sea as they were for such long stretches of time. If nothing else it would buy me time.

Calico's face flashed through my mind. Those blue eyes. Hurt; angry.

'Get out of my head,' I muttered.

'What?'

'Nothing.' I used the wall of the brig to pull myself to my feet. My knee was still badly bruised but the binding had done some good and I could put a little weight on it now. I curled my fingers around the bars at the door and stared out at Read.

Annie. Do you love me?

Ah, Calico. I came to sea with you, didn't I?

'Do you want to hear a secret?' I asked Read.

He raised an eyebrow.

'Come here.'

Read tipped his head back and laughed. The sound was unexpected, light, warm. 'You must take me for a fool. I like your boldness, little fellow, but I will not let you strangle me or put out my eyes, or whatever it is you plan.'

'If I did any of those things I'd be dead long before Jamaica,' I said. 'I just don't want to be heard by anyone else.'

He picked up his stool and dragged it a few inches closer, still staying well clear of the bars.

I kept my voice low. 'I lied to your captain,' I said. 'My name is not Ned Fletcher.'

His expression did not change but he leaned forward. 'I guessed as much.'

I stiffened but before I could ask what he meant a sharp sound rang out from the deck. A yelp. Read's eyes narrowed but he stayed seated. Another sound and this time I identified it as the crack of a lash against flesh. A curse was bitten off by another blow.

'Our captain is fond of floggings,' Read murmured. 'As you may find out for yourself.'

'What did you mean, you guessed as much?'

'Only a fool would give his real name.' But I wondered if there was more to it than that. I didn't like the sharpness of his gaze. The silence between us was only broken by the wet sound of the lash on flesh.

'I need to piss,' I said at last. 'Turn around.'

Read snorted. 'A shy pirate?'

'It's one thing in front of your shipmates and another in a cell in front of a guard. Turn around or I won't be able to go.'

'Odd little fellow.' But to my relief he turned around anyway and sat with his back to me. I used the bucket and put it aside, dragging my breeches up and lacing them.

'So what is it?' he asked.

'I'm done, you can turn around now. What is what?'

'If your name isn't Ned Fletcher, what is it?'

I shrugged. 'Only a fool would give his real name.'

A smile flashed across Read's face.

'Good,' he said. 'You may survive yet.'

12

BARNET

It was no great victory to capture some cabin boy, Barnet supposed. But even the most insignificant of men had a part to play. If nothing else he would have the boy tortured for information that might lead to the capture of the rest of his crew; perhaps others, since pirates were social creatures, forever consorting and conspiring with men of their ilk. The cabin boy was defiant now but Barnet wagered a few broken fingers and the threat of a hanging would loosen his tongue.

He sat in his cabin, going through the charts. Fifteen of his men had gone across to the *Kingston* to sail her in their wake. They would make port in Cuba and deposit the *Kingston,* along with the cabin boy. He would let the crew loose for a few days and take the extra time to careen the *Albion.* In his pursuit of the pirates he had neglected the upkeep of his vessel. Once that was rectified, he would take his own crew out to sea once more, seeking John Rackham and his people.

The women, screaming. Constance—

Barnet slowed. The memory had come upon him like a breaking wave, icy and sudden. A warm spot of pain moved behind his eyes and crept across his skull. The long chase was catching up with him. He would be glad of the rest in Cuba. Glad of fresh food, and sleep.

Constance—

Barnet finished going through the charts and stored them carefully in wooden cylinders with wax caps; charts were of great value and he had paid handsomely for these. He took off his coat and pinned his sleeves up at the elbow. He was not a man who enjoyed violence, but he conceded its necessity.

He went below to the brig, where Martin Read was perched on a stool with his feet propped against the bars. He swung them down and stood as Barnet approached.

'Captain,' he said.

'Open the brig,' Barnet ordered.

The prisoner scrambled to his feet. A skinny boy of about fourteen, with pointed features and impish green eyes. His hair would have been bright red if it wasn't darkened by dirt. Barnet felt contempt rise in him. Just another filthy pirate. Godless. Defiant. Murderous.

He was not, ordinarily, a man who enjoyed violence. He suspected this might be an exception.

13
BONNY

Barnet was going to hurt me. He had shed his stiff jacket and rolled his sleeves up. Since I had been put in the brig my mind had conjured all manner of glinting torture devices but Barnet's clenched fists reminded me a man does not need much imagination to inflict pain, and fear rolled through me unchecked.

Read came to the door of the brig. I backed away to the far side of the cell. What would Read do if I rushed Barnet? I looked over at the tall sailor. He avoided my gaze as he fiddled with the lock.

'Hurry up, man,' Barnet snapped.

'The lock is stiff, sir,' Read said. 'The salt.'

'Stand out of the way.' Barnet shouldered past Read and turned the key in the lock. It seemed to offer him no resistance.

Read stood away and met my gaze, his face grave. No. I couldn't expect any help from him. If he tried to intervene he would suffer the consequences, and it wouldn't do me any good. If the situation had been reversed, if he had been on our ship, would I have stayed Calico's hand? Of course not.

Barnet stepped into the brig. I could stand but I didn't trust my leg to take much if it came to a fight.

What did I have? What could I use?

As he reached forward I ducked under his arm and tried to go for the door. My knee buckled. I wasn't fast enough. He grabbed me. Air hissed in and out between my teeth. My body was coiled, expecting a blow, ready for the pain.

'Sir.'

'What?' Barnet's voice was a tight snarl and I realised how much he *wanted* to hurt me. Old Dad was right about this man. His hatred of pirates was gut-deep.

What did I have? What could I use?

'Sir, I think you should reconsider.'

My first instinct was to jam my elbow into Barnet's gut and take the opportunity to run for it, but I knew I wouldn't get far. I looked at Read. His dark eyes were steady.

'Tell him,' he said. 'Tell the captain what you are.'

He knew.

Perhaps he had known from the beginning.

What did I have? What could I use? Only what I was.

'I'm not a boy,' I said. My voice cracked. It was so strange to speak this out loud, to admit it to anyone except Calico. 'I'm a woman.'

Barnet's grip slackened on my arm. I pulled free and stumbled back a few steps. My hands were shaking. I hated myself for being so afraid.

'A woman?' Barnet hissed. His hand tightened on me again and he whipped around to face Read. 'You knew?'

'I suspected, sir. When she asked me to turn so she could…' He coughed. 'I suspected.'

The pirate hunter's face twisted. 'Then you are Anne Bonny,' he said.

I caught my breath.

My name.

How did they know my name?

Barnet shook me until my teeth knocked together and when he released me I almost fell against the bars. I caught them. Steadied myself. Barnet slammed the door of the brig closed. His eyes were hard and angry. For now, some corrupted sense of chivalry kept him from hurting me.

'So, you've heard of me.' I tried to keep my tone

flippant. It would have worked if I could have caught my breath, but I was still giddy from the shaking.

'You will stay in this brig until we reach Cuba,' Barnet snarled, as if I hadn't spoken. 'There, you will face justice. If the courts see fit, Anne Bonny, you will still hang. And if not, I will see you returned to your husband with a lesson that will dog you until the end of your sorry days.'

The world around me was so quiet, so still. If Barnet was waiting for a reaction, I could not give him one. I just stood there, frozen, until he growled in disgust and turned on his heel. His boots clipped against the wooden planks. The sound echoed.

I had been running from my husband for months. And now, it seemed, I was sailing right into his grasp.

'I met your husband, you know.'

Read's words came to me as if through water. I had forgotten he was even there. I didn't remember sitting down but I had to look up to see his face.

'What?'

'I met your husband.' He pulled up his stool and took a seat again. 'Back in Jamaica.'

I wanted to say something sharp but couldn't call anything to mind. Memories of James Bonny slowed and weighed me down. I set my jaw.

Read's tone was neutral. 'Did he hurt you?'

A laugh bubbled up in my throat and I leaned my brow against the wall of the brig and kept laughing until my lungs hurt. By the time I ran out of breath my head was spinning. I pushed back my hair and raised my eyes to Read.

'Yes,' he said. 'I thought as much.' He rested his elbows on his knees. 'Why did you marry him?'

'Why do you care?'

He frowned but didn't answer.

'He wasn't always a brute,' I said at last. 'He was quite charming, once. Talked about freedom. Brought me gifts. A knife, a pistol. How did you know I was a woman?'

He shrugged. 'A guess, mostly. I knew there was a red-headed Irish woman on Rackham's ship. I was surprised the captain did not see it for himself. Perhaps he expected your disguise to be less convincing.'

'Why didn't you tell him straight away? What do you get out of this, Read?'

He took some hardtack out of his pocket, dusted it off, and started trying to chip little bits off with his teeth.

'Call it a whim,' he said at last. 'I have my own views on Captain Barnet.'

'Why did you join?'

A strange look passed over his face. 'I was out of work after the war. For a while I ran an inn. But such a life was not meant for me, and so I came to the sea. I sailed when I was a boy, and the pay is sufficient.'

'You were a soldier?' On any other day I wouldn't have been interested in my captor's life, but I really didn't want to think about my husband. I clung to the distraction.

'In Flanders. The good Charles Habsburg had the gall to die without an heir. Half of Europe entered the struggle.'

'Did your side win?'

'It was a war.' His lips tipped. 'No one wins.'

'Mister Read?'

The voice belonged to a scrawny boy coming down the companionway. He had a black eye and no shirt but when he saw Read his face split into a wide grin. He dropped onto the planks next to the man and handed him a mug. He couldn't have been older than ten.

'No more coffee,' he said, 'but the bumbo is good.' A hot drink of rum, water, sugar and nutmeg. Calico always added lime as well.

'Thank you, Oliver.' Read handed the boy another hardtack from his pocket. They sat dipping the biscuits into the mug. The normalcy of the scene helped to shake away the shadow of James Bonny. I forced myself to edge forward and wrap my fingers about the bars of the brig. I wasn't hungry but I knew I needed my strength.

'Feel like sharing?' I asked.

The boy glanced at me, then looked at Read. Read shrugged and dug around in his pocket for another biscuit. He passed it through the bars to me.

'How many of those do you *have*?' the boy asked.

Read just winked and held out the mug to me. The bumbo warmed my stomach. I wondered, briefly, whether there was any way I could upend it onto Read, scald him, and somehow get to the keys. But where would I go? Besides, he was the only thing keeping the crew from me. I dipped the hardtack, soaking it so it had a little flavour and didn't break my teeth. The food was enough to restore some of my spirit.

'The captain said you're a woman,' Oliver blurted out at last. News got around fast.

Read, with the mug at his lips, snorted and spilled some. 'God's blood, Oliver.'

'Your captain's right,' I said.

'That mean you don't get hung?'

Read nudged the boy, who looked indignant. 'What? She's a prisoner, we don't get to ask her questions?'

'Hanged,' I said. I wasn't bothered by the query.

Oliver blinked at me. 'Well? Do you get hanged, then?'

'Women can get hanged just as much as men.' I shrugged. 'If they try me, and convict me, I'll go to the gallows.'

'They won't convict you though. Because you're a woman.'

'They might.' I could probably wriggle out of the piracy charges, but it was damning that I had left my husband for Calico. It was bitter to know that even now my fate was bound to my husband's.

'Don't you *care?*'

'There are worse things than execution. If the choice is between a hanging and going back to my husband, I'll dance the hempen jig with a wide smile on my face.'

Read turned his steady gaze to me and did not say a word. There was no way of telling what was going through his mind.

I didn't have to be up on the deck to know when we arrived in Havana. I could feel it in the shift of the waters around us, hear it in the sounds of the gulls and the vendors on the docks. I was almost grateful. I was dirty and greasy. The baby in my belly was still upsetting my innards and the brig stank of vomit, though Read had been decent enough to bring me fresh water each day, and Oliver had changed the buckets every time it was needed. If Read thought it odd that my stomach rebelled so often he didn't say so. I grew accustomed to his watchful quiet and to Oliver's curious chatter.

I was a mouthy little shit on the *Ranger*. But now I tried to follow Read's example. I had to focus on what came ahead.

I had options. I couldn't let my fear of James Bonny cloud my mind. There was still a lot of time and distance between the *Albion* and the trial. I would have to take any opportunity for escape. Try to make my way to Calico's friends, the Cunninghams. Have the baby, leave it with them, go back to sea.

If I didn't escape before the trial I could plead my belly. A pregnant woman couldn't be hanged—it was seen as tantamount to murder—so I'd get a stay of execution until the baby was born. Another seven months or so. Plenty of time to work on the guards and find a way out.

'We'll be docked soon,' Read said, coming down to the brig after his off-shift. Oliver, half-asleep on the stool, jerked upright and tried to look alert. He skirted around Read and scrambled up the companionway, presumably to get a good look at the port of Havana as we approached. Read came to the door of the brig and studied me.

'Thinking about how much you'll miss me?' I asked.

He did not smile. 'The captain will not risk taking you down the docks himself,' he said. 'He believes you are likely to cause some form of disturbance.'

'I wonder why.'

'He will bring soldiers. They will come onto the ship and take you away.'

I stood and went to the bars. His fingers were wrapped around them. I set my hands just below his and brought my face closer.

'They will take you to trial. To the gallows, or back to your husband.'

'Yes.' Every muscle in my body was tense. Was he going to help me?

'Read!' someone called from above. 'Come get your pay!'

He rapped the bars twice, and went to the upper decks. I watched him go. Tall, broad-shouldered, his stride easy and long. Was he wiping me from his mind? I'd had the strangest feeling he was almost about to throw his lot in with me.

I paced the length of the brig. I didn't have to bend as much as the other men at this level but I still had to bow my head as I walked back and forth.

There were always options.

My mind was made up by the time Read returned with a purse at his hip. I would tell him I was with child. He was a decent man, and decent men couldn't resist a woman in distress. It might tip him the rest of the way, might sway him in favour of helping me to escape.

I never had the chance. He came back to the bars and leaned in. His voice was low.

'The rest of the crew leaves to spend their money and have a night of freedom,' he said. 'We will move when they are gone, so be ready.'

For a moment I couldn't speak. Couldn't push my mind past this strangeness. Why would he help me? What did he have to gain? And did I trust him?

I didn't have time for doubt. I had to take the chance.

'Thank you.'

'Don't let on. Be ready.'

I struggled to keep my voice level. 'Always.'

14

BONNY

Night darkened all corners of the ship. I couldn't shut off the nerves that twitched my body. My eyes flicked into nooks and shadows and my ears pricked with the slightest sound. The vessel groaned. The waves were muted against the hull, but I could hear them, the constant push and rasp I had lived with for the last few months. It was like a lullaby. I was twelve when we left Ireland, me and my parents, and sailed to Charles Town. I remembered sitting below with my mother, listening to her croon in harmony with the tides. I sought solace in the memory now, some kind of calm centre, but there was no comfort in it. Even then, my mother had been sickly.

She died a few months after we landed.

Shadows danced on the wall of the brig, threaded through the imprint of the bars. There was a lamp at the top of the companionway and every so often I saw men moving past. They lugged barrels and sacks and clattered down the steps. I strained my ears listening for the sound of guns and swords. Barnet would be there soon; I would be dragged off the ship and into a cell. There would be no hope for me then.

Read was catlike as he finally descended the stairs.

'You took your time,' I hissed, weak with relief.

'I had to be sure the others were out of the way.' He turned the key in the lock and pulled the door open.

'Did you bring me a gun?'

He narrowed his eyes. 'I've seen you shoot.'

'I'd be an idiot to shoot *you*.'

He hesitated, then passed me a flintlock. I tested the weight in my hand. My fear swept away. Was there a more invincible feeling than being freshly armed?

'That smile concerns me. Let's go.' Read went first. He went quiet for such a tall man, soft-footed and careful. I followed him. I didn't have time to pause and enjoy the fresh air, the cool touch of the wind on my cheek, but I savoured it.

The *Albion* was gentle in the Havana harbour, swaying and knocking on the jetty. Once we were on the open decks Read ducked, keeping low to avoid being seen from the shore. I stooped as well. We didn't go to the gangplank but instead to the seaward side of the ship. Read had secured a rope ladder to the stern. When I leaned over, I saw a small boat waiting, secured by a line.

'You don't do things by halves, do you?' I whispered.

'You first. Go.'

My leg was still stiff from the bruising a few days before but it was better than it had been. I swung myself over the rail and climbed down the rope ladder, letting my arms take most of my weight. I eased myself into the boat and couldn't help reaching into the salt water, splashing it over my face. After days in the brig, the water was a luxury.

Read followed. He wasn't as comfortable in the ropes as me, but he was strong and sure.

'Mister Read!'

He stopped halfway. Looked up at Oliver, peering over the rail at us. His face was pale in the dim light of the ship lanterns.

Read kept climbing. 'Come with us,' he said.

Oliver drew back. 'My mum got me this job,' he hissed.

'Come on, Oliver.'

'I send her back money.'

'We'll find a new job.'

Oliver shook his head and backed away. He disappeared from the railing without another word. Read dropped into the boat. It was too dark to see his face but the silence between us was taut.

Read waited. I think he was hoping for Oliver to change his mind and swing over the railing. But there was no sign of the boy and soon we saw torches flickering on the jetty. Read took a breath, then an oar.

'Will he be all right?' I asked, my eyes tracking back to the ship.

Read lowered his head. 'Just row,' he said.

We went without lamp or light, our boat slipping between the ships in silence. We rowed slowly, careful of the movement of our oars in the water. When we pulled clear of hulls we kept our heads low, and from the *Albion* to the shore neither of us said another word. My heart kept up a strange double-stutter the whole way. I remembered, in a brief flash of delight and fear, the night I fled my husband. Dodging the shadows in Nassau. Terrified he would come after me. Terrified I would stumble upon rowdy pirates. Wild and frantic by the time I found Calico. Sobbing in his arms, breathless and shaking because no one had ever kissed me so gently.

Annie. Do you love me?

Ah, Calico. I came to sea with you, didn't I?

And I locked those thoughts away because where was Calico now? The only trace of him was the baby in my belly.

We didn't tie the boat but we dragged it up the beach and shoved it alongside two others. I had never been to Cuba before. Even in the moonlight I could see that Havana was a pale city, sandy and sparse, holding back the thick trees that hedged in from further inland. Without a crew behind me, only Read at my side, it seemed impossibly big. And Cunningham was a common enough name, even in a Spanish port. I wished that Calico and I had taken the time to go through the details.

But I was out in the clear air and I had an ally. Even if I couldn't begin to guess his motives.

We stole up along the beach towards the dirt track to the city. Neither of us said a word.

I sat in a corner of a tavern draped in Read's large jacket and ate some dried beef. It wasn't much but it was more than I'd had on the ship and my stomach was grateful. I watched Read as he leaned on the bar, his manner casual, easy. As if he had lived all his life on the docks of Havana and had known these men for years. Money changed hands. Bribes of silence, I guessed. I pushed back the questions that surged through my mind. Why was he helping me? What did he want?

He strolled back with hot drinks and more food. I wasn't sure exactly what the food was. Beans; some sort of meat.

'Some of the men had suggestions,' Read said. 'I have enough pay to last us out a few weeks, but I'd rather not use it up if we can go to ground safely. Do you trust these Cunninghams?'

'I don't know them.'

'Do you trust the man who sent you to them?'

I caught my breath and faltered. Did I?

'Yes,' I said. The word came out strong.

'Then that is our best option.' He drank from his mug and sat back, brow tucking as he thought. 'Eat quickly, then we start searching.'

We ate in silence. I wanted to ask all my questions but I didn't. I doubted I would get answers.

Once we were done with our meal we went out into the streets of Havana. 'In Havana, by the port,' was all Calico had told me, and it wasn't a lot to go on. I thought I remembered him talking about them before. What was the husband, a stevedore? A fisherman or a cooper?

'One of the men back there knows a fisherman called Cunningham,' Read said, as if reading my thoughts. 'We'll start there.'

The fisherman wasn't the Cunningham we were looking for but he had an uncle who was a merchant and a cousin who was a stevedore. Read and I debated quietly for a short while but in the end he deferred to my half-memory and we went to find the stevedore. He lived in a small house by the harbour with sturdy walls and a brick-tile roof. Not the house of a rich man, but a real house all the same. It was much more than I had shared with James Bonny on Nassau. I stood in front of the door for a few breaths, trying to summon the courage to knock. Finally Read leaned over my shoulder and did it for me. I couldn't say why I had hesitated.

It was a woman who answered the door. She was tall and fat and beautiful, with brown eyes and more freckles than I had ever seen on another person. She folded her arms and leaned against the doorframe. Her eyes were swollen from sleep and she wore a man's old coat over her nightclothes.

'No beggars,' she said.

'We are not beggars, ma'am.' Read's rough voice belied his manners. 'We come from a man named Calico Jack.'

The woman's eyes narrowed. 'So you say. Who are you?'

I weakened with relief. 'My name is Anne Bonny. I'm—'

'Calico's girl,' she finished, her shoulders relaxing, and I felt a twitch of annoyance. I was young but I wasn't anyone's girl.

'He wrote you?' My mind flipped over the numbers. How could a letter have reached Havana so fast? Where had he sent it from? Who had delivered it?

'Wrote us? No, he was here two days back.'

The news hit me like a marlinespike. I lost my breath. *Here two days back.* 'Is he still in port?'

'No. He shipped out yesterday on the morning tide. Said if by some miracle you showed up on our doorstep, we should take you in.' Her eyes flicked to Read. '…He didn't say anything about *this* fellow.'

Yesterday. I had missed him by a crossing of the sun. My lungs felt like they had caved in.

I choked back my disappointment. 'This fellow saved my life.' I hesitated. 'And the life of Calico's child.'

Read stiffened. I almost grinned at the blank shock on his face. Felt good to give him a turn, when he was always so calm. He'd gone pale. I wondered if he was realising, in that moment, exactly what sort of a fate he'd saved me from when he stopped Barnet from beating me.

'Hmm. Calico mentioned that too.' She studied me a moment more, then stepped aside. 'Better come in, both of you. I'm Rose Cunningham. My man Walter's out but he'll be back soon enough. How far along are you?'

'It'll be close to three months now. Far as I can tell. I'm not a midwife.'

'A half-drowned rat is what you are.' Her broad face crinkled as we passed. 'And you smell like one too, dear. You'd best get yourself cleaned before you take to any of my fresh linens. Do you have clothes to spare?'

'Nothing but what I'm wearing.'

'Well, mine won't fit you very well but we'll have to make do. And as your belly grows that might be for the best.' She rounded on Read before he was even properly inside. 'And you. Mind your manners. No messing around or there'll be a reckoning, do you understand? I don't care if you're a pirate or a brigand or the King himself. You'll keep civil under my roof.'

'Yes, ma'am.' Read had gathered himself enough to answer, and he slipped back into his easy way like it was nothing. Still, I felt his eyes on me. Reassessing. Turning it over in that quiet mind of his.

'Why didn't you say?' Read waited until Rose was in the next room, boiling hot water, before he spoke. He was supposed to be in the next room changing his clothes and I was supposed to be changing mine but instead we stood at the door and whispered to one another.

'What would it have helped?'

'I never would have let Barnet come so close to...' He clamped his mouth shut. 'I would have brought you more food, anyway.'

His concern made me uncomfortable. It was the first time he had treated me like a woman, I realised. Like other men treated women. Like I couldn't be trusted to make my own decisions. 'No harm done.'

'You could have come to a *good deal* of harm.'

I shrugged and retreated further into the room,

grabbing Rose's large clothes. I didn't much care if Read saw me, not now that all my secrets were in the open. I stripped and used a wet flannel and a bucket of warm water to quickly scrub off the worst of the dirt. When I turned back, I realised Read had quietly closed the door and taken to his own room. I grinned at the thought of Martin Read, sailor and soldier, so tall and imposing, gone shy.

I cracked the door a few moments later. He whipped around, doing up the laces at the front of the shirt Rosa had given him.

'Knock,' Read said curtly.

'Calm down, it's nothing I haven't seen before.' I stepped into the room and noticed his muscles tightening, his face becoming guarded and taut. 'Are you going to stay here?' I asked.

'Only until I find a job at the docks,' he replied. 'Maybe further west than here. Once the *Albion* is out of the harbour and it's safe, I'll take another room.'

It felt strange, to talk about parting. Much had happened in a short time.

'And you?' he asked. 'When you…will you stop here to have the child?'

'I don't have much choice, do I?'

'Where will you go after?'

'Back to our ship.' I said it with more certainty than I felt. 'Back to Calico.'

'Do you miss him?'

Calico's blue eyes. The flash of his coat as he walked across a deck. It was so easy to want him when he wasn't around, I thought wryly. When we couldn't bicker or disagree or misunderstand one another. My heart skittered at the thought of him but I tried to keep my mind clear.

'I'll live.'

'That was not the question.'

I shook my head. I had maybe six long months ahead of me before I could even think of going back to Calico and the crew. 'You don't…' I trailed off as a loud clamour sounded outside. I felt my heart speed, my hands dampen. A flash of memory shot across me: Nassau at night, overrun with pirates, drunkards, violence. I wanted to go to the window but I couldn't make myself move. In the end it was Read who crossed the room and glanced out.

'Looks like Barnet's knocked up a crowd,' he said. He looked over his shoulder at me. 'You'll have to stay indoors for a few days at least. The captain is a proud man. He doesn't like to lose.'

'That could be said for all of us.' I tried to ignore the sounds on the docks. We were safe for now. I wouldn't leave the house until Barnet was back at sea.

I hesitated, then finally asked the question that had been on my mind since Read let me out of the brig. 'Why did you help me?'

Read pulled the shutters across and stepped away from the window. He leaned against the wall and shrugged.

'No single reason,' he said. 'I have not been easy with Captain Barnet's methods for some time. And the crew...' His jaw hardened. 'They are hard men, with a hard purpose. I suppose that was to be expected, but I had thought to see some honour there, too. I did not think I would find myself completely alone with a crew of louts and thugs.'

That made sense to me. I had spent the last few months sailing with louts and thugs, but at least they never pretended to be anything else. They didn't try to justify it with King and Country.

'But I was sorry to leave Oliver behind,' Read reflected. 'It will not be easy for him. Still, I never planned to stay long on the *Albion*.'

I had more questions but I sensed this was an end to Read's answers.

'Thank you,' I said at last.

He shrugged again but I reached over and caught his arm. 'Read. Thank you. I have met few decent men. You're one of them.'

I didn't wear sincerity well. It felt uncomfortable and stiff.

As Read opened his mouth to reply, there was a crash. A shout, fists hammering on the door. We both jumped into action. He blew out the candle and we took up our weapons, standing on either side of the door, pressed against the wall.

The banging on the door continued. I breathed hard. My eyes fixed on Read, standing opposite me. His face was tense and his eyes were focused, dark. An unexpected twist of guilt upset my stomach. I had called him a decent man. What had I pulled this decent man into?

'My husband isn't here!' Rose's voice rose through over the commotion. 'What do you mean by all this?'

'Out of the way.'

'I won't let you in.' She spoke with all the authority of a general at war, her words cracking out over the chatter and murmur of men.

'Stand aside!'

'Don't touch me!'

Someone was going to be killed. Could I stand by and let it happen? I wasn't going to hand myself in. Maybe we could get out through the window, get out before it could escalate.

The door clapped open again.

'What is all of this?' A man shouted over it all. 'Let go of my wife. How dare you!'

This must be Walter Cunningham, I thought.

'We are here seeking wanted criminals.' I recognised the other voice. It was Barnet's bosun, a solid man named Hutch. 'Your wife refuses to stand aside.'

'Of course she does! We are respectable people! Is it your habit to manhandle women, sir? Are you a gentleman?'

A silence, and I realised after a moment that it was a *shamed* silence. I could hardly believe it.

'I can assure you there are no criminals in this house,' Cunningham went on. 'By all means, come inside and make an inspection. But I will be taking my complaints to your captain.'

There was some shuffling and a deal of muttering. Someone came inside. Cunningham didn't know we were there, I thought. Were we in trouble? Read cocked his gun.

Footsteps near the door.

'Walter!' Rose's voice, cracking with distress. 'Will you let them into our personal rooms? These strange men, in our bedroom? My underclothes—'

'All seems to be in order.' Hutch spoke hurriedly, and the footsteps retreated. There was some more quiet conversation and Cunningham promised to give assistance if he caught any trace of us. Then the door closed and quiet fell.

I slid down against the wall, relief making me light-headed. I rested a hand on my belly, on the child, wondering if the fluttering there was me or it. The Cunninghams talked quietly on the other side of the door, then Rose cracked it open.

'It's safe,' she said.

Walter Cunningham joined her in the threshold. He was a chubby man with bright eyes and a warm smile. He laughed when he saw me. 'Oh yes,' he said. 'You're *exactly* Calico's fancy, aren't you?'

'That was a close thing,' I said, ignoring his comment as Read helped me to my feet.

'All thunder, no lightning,' Cunningham said. 'They're gone now, and that's what matters. Welcome, Anne.' He nodded to Read. 'Thank you for delivering her safely to us,' he said and I felt a flicker of irritation at the tone. Read met my gaze, his lips quirking. He obviously felt the dismissal in Cunningham's words. He extended a hand to me.

'Anne Bonny,' he said. 'It has been a pleasure.'

I took his hand. His grip was warm, rough with calluses. I didn't want him to go.

'They're searching tonight. You need to stay at least until they sail.'

A smile flitted across his face. 'Thousands of harbour rats live here in Havana, Bonny,' he said. 'What is one more? They can search. They will not find me.'

Across the days stuck in Barnet's brig, during our escape in Cuba, I had found myself enjoying Read's company. I couldn't remember the last time I'd had a real friend. And though the Cunninghams were friends of Calico's, they were strangers to me. Strangers who lived a land-locked life I could not understand.

'Goodbye, Read,' I said. How could I thank him? How could I even begin?

I watched as Read took his gun and his bag. Kept watching as he slung them over his shoulders and stole out the door.

15
BARNET

So: they were gone. Read and the woman, in the dead of night.

Barnet had had the boy Oliver soundly beaten. He sobbed and whimpered like the pup he was but had no helpful information. Apparently he had come out onto the deck just in time to see the boat disappearing between two other ships in the harbour. Whether they had gone ashore or found another ship Barnet did not know. He would do his best to find out but Havana was the third-largest city in the Americas. People drifted in and out with the tides and he knew it would be, for the most part, a futile effort.

But he had offered a reward and word had spread, and a dozen drunk sailors and their whores had been brought to him. No sign of Bonny or Read.

Now he paced the length of the *Albion*. Barnet was a man of decision, unaccustomed to uncertainty. The deck was always shifting beneath his feet but the rest of his world was fixed: God and England. King and Country. An end to all pirates.

His treacherous mind crept now towards the fire and fear that had given him his purpose. *The roar of guns, the screams of women. The breath that snarled in his chest as he pressed into the shadows and prayed to God for mercy.*

Shaken, he cast the thoughts from his mind. That was long years ago, and he was a better man now. He could not allow the shadow of the past to bring him to his knees. Barnet turned on his heel and went along the deck. His hands were locked behind his back to keep them from shaking. No crewman would see weakness on his bearing, but he was torn.

His baser instinct was to stay in Havana, to pursue this godless woman and the man who had betrayed him. The woman might be bait to Rackham—but maybe not. Perhaps she meant nothing to him, and he had already moved on to another whore. It was not worth the risk. Staying to hunt out Bonny and Read would mean neglecting his pursuit of the rest of the horde. He had a responsibility, and a duty. He had a commission.

'Captain?' Johnson, a stout fellow who had taken over as the main helmsman, stood straighter as his captain approached. He was carrying a coil of rope but he set it down and stood with his hands respectfully held behind his back. Johnson had once been a military man. He knew how to treat a captain with respect.

'We leave on the morning tide,' Barnet said.

'And our bearing, sir?'

'We sail for New Providence Island.' He might not find Rackham in Nassau, the port city of New Providence, but he would find the governor, Woodes Rogers—a man committed to stamping out piracy. If Barnet was to receive any sort of aid, he would find it there.

16
BONNY

Time rolled in and out like the breakers. Calico was off in the wide world somewhere and all I could do was count the tides until I could join him. Read took a job as a stevedore. I saw him every now and again on the docks, rolling barrels and smoking pipes with the other dock-lads. Sometimes our eyes met. He would smile and nod and walk on. I think he felt that the Cunninghams mistrusted him, and he had no wish to linger around them.

It was a loss. Read was one of the few people who had ever known it all and still treated me like a person. Calico, too; but it was complicated with Calico. Read, although I had only known him for a short time, was my friend.

Not that there was anything wrong with Walter and Rose Cunningham. Calico had grown up with Walter. He had a quiet, wicked sense of humour that I knew Calico would warm to. Rose was like a small hurricane, rattling from one end of the house to another, always on the move. I liked her. Formidable women reminded me of my mother, who during her life had never settled for anything less than exactly what she wanted.

Everyone else seemed to like Rose, too. She had a frank, comical way of talking that drew people to her. As a result there was a constant stream of people through the house during the day. They came to sew and cook and talk and I couldn't possibly hide. Eventually Rose put about that I was her cousin, left in a bad way by a careless sailor. The other women clucked their tongues and side-eyed me. Some of them asked uncomfortable questions, but soon their interest died. Either they knew intuitively that Rose would be raising the child, or she had spoken to them quietly about it. It quelled the questions and the gossip—and kept me safe, for the time being, from the rumours and questions that floated along the docks under Barnet's directive. It also meant I had to sit and sew with them. A few years before, when I lived in my father's house in Charles Town, I would have seen sewing as unendurable torture. I still didn't enjoy it, but at least I was safe. Safe and bored.

I wished Calico was there. He would have made it fun. He would have teased me, insulted me, brought me food or pretty things from the market on the hard days. It should have been both of us marking my impressive girth, or counting the number of times I had to get up in the night and piss.

The thought made me morose. I knew there were many women who were left behind in ports while their men went off to sea. I'd just never thought I would be one of them.

I sat on a jetty one afternoon, seven months along, watching the ships and feeling the insistent wriggle and kick of Calico's baby. Rose had told me she was sure it was a girl from the way it sat. I hoped not. I would find it much harder to leave a girl, even though I knew the Cunninghams would do their best for her. The world was no place for girls.

Shaking my head, I laced my fingers across my stomach. The child would be fine, girl or boy. I would sail away and not look back. I had been doing it all my life. It ran in my family, after all. My father had always been good at cutting his losses.

'Hungry?'

I jolted. Martin Read sat himself down beside me, barefoot and comfortable in breeches and a loose shirt. He'd clearly been working in the sun for most of the time since I'd seen him last. Bitterness twisted in me. I'd had to wear Rose's old clothes for months. They were heavy and hot and I preferred a man's garb. I put my envy aside for a moment.

'It's been a while,' I said.

'Been busy.' He handed me a banana.

'Too busy to visit the criminal you freed and ran away with?'

He shrugged, as if that was a reply, and fished into his pocket for his pipe and tobacco.

'Five months and scarcely a nod, and now we're having lunch together?' I peeled the banana in any case and took a bite. 'What's the occasion, Read?'

He lit the pipe. 'You look well,' he said, ignoring my question. 'And fat.'

I laughed through my mouthful. I really *liked* this strange, secretive man who had saved my life. I didn't even mind that he dodged my questions and wanted to float in and out of my life like driftwood.

'Are you on your own?' he asked. From another man the question would have triggered unease. Not from Read.

'No.' I nodded over my shoulder. 'Rose and Walter are haggling over fishing tackle. Or rice, or something like that. I couldn't stand it much longer so I came away to watch the ships.'

'Not suited for domesticity, are you?'

I shrugged. 'Short life and a merry one, isn't that what they say?'

'Who says that?'

'I don't know. Pirates, probably.'

He snorted. 'Have you heard from your captain yet?'

My smile faded. 'No. I still can't believe I only missed him by *one day*. Wretched timing.' I had lamented this to Rose and Walter until they were tired of hearing it. 'Would it have killed him to wait for me just a day longer?'

'It might have.'

I hated how true it was. 'I know, I know. It's just lonely.' The words surprised me. When had I ever complained of being lonely?

He shrugged again. 'For me, also.'

I glanced at him. 'What?'

'Is this such a surprise?'

'There's a profound difference between you and me, Read: I'm a mouthy little bastard, and you're not. You play nice—I wouldn't think you'd have too much trouble making friends.'

He seemed amused but didn't comment, blowing out rings of smoke. 'Come for a walk?' he said at last.

'Let me tell the Cunninghams first, or they'll pine for me.'

Rose and Walter weren't thrilled by the notion of me walking off with a man who was still a stranger to them, but over the months they had come to understand how long I could hold an argument. They asked me to be back before dark—I told them I would consider it—and then I joined Read strolling along the docks.

'They seem like reasonable people,' Read said. 'Decent.'

They were. No wonder I felt lonely.

'So where are we going?'

He just grinned. I had a passing moment of doubt. I didn't like putting myself in someone else's hands. I trusted Read but I had trusted people before, and where were they now? My father was somewhere in Charles Town, childless. My husband was somewhere in Nassau, hating me, wanting me back just to hurt me. And who knew where Calico was? Somewhere out on the wild sea, if he was still alive.

The worst thing about being pregnant, and there were many bad things, was that I had to stop and be alone with my thoughts for such a stretch of time.

Read led me to a small wooden building by the rocky shore, away from the wild buzz of the city centre. The land cut off sharply there, with a drop about as tall as I was. Several small boats bobbed in the water, tied to a rickety jetty that stretched over the waves. There was a carpentry bench out in the sun, and several half-finished projects scattered around.

I could hear music and loud laughter, male laughter, and my first instinct was to pull back and return to the

Cunninghams. If I'd been dressed as a boy I wouldn't have minded but it was a different matter when I was in skirts. Then I heard women laughing as well and some of the tension left my shoulders.

We rounded the corner. A small group was sitting around with drinks and food. A stocky, bearded young man was playing a fiddle; he looked over and grinned as we approached but he didn't stop playing.

'These are the musicians and players of the *Jeremiah and Anne,*' Read said. 'They're here for a few weeks, awaiting orders.'

'Orders from whom?'

'Bartholomew Roberts.'

I froze before we reached them. 'What?'

Bartholomew Roberts was the best pirate on the sea. Bar none. The Welshman caught more ships in his career than Blackbeard ever had. He had a whole *fleet.*

'They don't…look like Roberts' men.'

'How did you expect Roberts' men to look?'

'Less fun. How do you know them?'

'Read's been loading and unloading for us these past few months,' the fiddler said, cutting in on us. He drew the bow across the string to finish the song and stood, extending a hand to me. 'Darling.'

I raised an eyebrow. 'Steady on. We've just met.'

'This is Willum Darling,' Read said. 'Darling, this is Anne Bonny.'

I felt I would never get used to hearing my full name. I had always been Anne to my husband, Annie to Jack, and Bonny to the crew and Read.

'Nice to know you, bonny Bonny.' He stood and let me have the stool. Usually I would have stood anyway, just to spite him, but my back ached and my feet were sore.

'And you, darling Darling,' I said, settling down. 'What's a musician doing with Black Bart's fleet?'

Darling shrugged and put his bow back to his fiddle. 'Captain likes music,' he said. 'What's a well-spoken lady like you doing with a grunt like Read?'

'I had some trouble with a fellow named Barnet,' I said. 'Read helped me out.'

'Jonathan Barnet?' Darling asked.

'You know him?'

'Of him. We've dodged him before but he's never chased us properly. Read, you used to work under him, aye?'

Read shrugged, already refilling his pipe. Smoking wasn't practical at sea where the risk of fire was so great, but Read seemed to be making up for the lost time.

'I heard he ran afoul of Blackbeard.' A blonde lass dropped onto Read's lap. Read didn't push her away but he looked like he wanted to.

'Blackbeard?' Darling snorted. 'No, Peggy. Edward Teach wasn't working the Charles Town round until just two years shy of his death. No, from what I hear Jonathan Barnet's grudge against our lot is longer and harder than anything Blackbeard could impress. Rumour has it he was a hand on a ship that got took by Henry Avery.'

The blonde woman cuddled up to Read, who ignored her.

'Who is Henry Avery?' he asked, clearly trying to divert her attention.

'Was. Well, we think so. Might be alive I suppose.' Darling answered for her. He was still playing, the bow tipping back and forth as music spun from the fiddle. 'He disappeared a few years ago, presumably taking his riches with him. He was a hard bastard, though.'

'So is Barnet,' I said.

'Makes sense. Anyhow, story goes that Barnet was a young fellow and Avery took the ship. Passenger ship, with women aboard. Tortured them all, murdered most of them, took everything they had. Barnet survived.'

'That would do it,' Read said. 'Shame settles deeper than anger.'

The blonde woman, bored, slid off his lap and went to find another man to tease.

'Plenty of people survive pirate attacks,' I said with a shrug. 'Doesn't mean they come after us like the Devil's cracking the lash.'

Darling cocked his head, a small smile parting his thick beard. 'Us?' he asked.

'Why did Barnet survive?' I asked.

'Who knows? Perhaps he made a deal with Avery's crew.'

Read snorted. 'Hardly,' he said. 'Not a man of compromise.'

'Ah, you'd be surprised,' Darling said, with the lofty wisdom of someone perhaps a year older than Read. 'Barnet would only have been a boy at the time. Fear can do funny things to a young 'un.'

I thought of my husband and couldn't argue.

17
BARNET

Governor Woodes Rogers was a stocky, strong-looking man. He was a sailor with a hard face and clear, clever eyes. He must have been forty years old or so, roughly the same age as Barnet himself. He came forward to meet Barnet and clasped his hand, almost as if they were equals.

'Captain Barnet,' he said. 'I hear you have been a champion of our particular cause. I am gratified to find a man so committed to the eradication of piracy in our waters.'

Barnet bowed slightly. He did not voice his private opinion that Woodes Rogers had been too lenient in offering pardons to this point. 'I am glad to do my part.'

'And you are currently in pursuit?'

'Yes, sir. John Rackham and his crew.'

A smile flickered across Rogers' lips. 'Ah,' he said.

'Sir?'

'I wonder, Captain Barnet, how much you know of this particular crew.'

'As it turns out, sir...' Barnet cleared his throat. 'For a while we had a captive. Unfortunately...she escaped.'

Rogers raised an eyebrow. 'Anne Bonny.'

Barnet stiffened. 'You know of her, sir?'

'We had an encounter. Not a woman to be taken lightly, I think. She is manipulative and cunning, Captain Barnet. I am not surprised she escaped you.'

'I believe she seduced one of my crewmen, who disappeared that same day.'

'I would not be surprised.' Rogers sat back, studying Barnet. 'So. How may I assist?'

'Men, sir, and arms,' Barnet said. 'We have pushed our funds and our rations in chasing these pirates. My crew grow thin and restless. Some have absconded already. With your assistance, however, I believe we can bring Calico Jack to heel. Make an example of him.'

Rogers steepled his hands. 'When I came to Nassau, the town was a lawless pit of drink, disease and debauchery,' he said.

Barnet knew this to be true. There had been no government; pirates had run everything. Rogers had forced order onto the town with little more than a few dedicated men and his will.

'I knew piracy had to be eradicated in order to bring trade and prosperity to New Providence Island. But I wonder what stirs you, Captain Barnet. It is not often we see men petitioning for a commission to hunt pirates. There is little profit in the endeavour. Before I commit finance or men to your cause I wish to know why.'

'I have seen first-hand the evil pirates bring upon the world, sir.' Barnet hoped this would suffice as an answer but Rogers just kept staring at him. 'The pirate Henry Avery, sir. I was a cabin boy.' His muscles were locked, so tense they ached. He clenched his jaw. He could still feel every strike and blow from the beating. He could still hear every scream. 'Avery was a man without honour. God spared me from a slow and bloody death. I must believe He did so for a reason. If that reason is to rid the ocean of piracy, then I will do my duty.'

Silence fell between them. It had been a long time since Barnet had spoken of Henry Avery. A headache roared through his skull.

Rogers sat forward and dipped a quill. 'Very well, Captain Barnet. You will have what you require.'

18
BONNY

Darling and the crew of the *Jeremiah and Anne* sailed out of Havana a month and a half later on a bleak Friday. I could feel a storm in the air but Darling just laughed, gave me a scratchy kiss on the cheek, clasped Read's hand, and left us. I wanted badly to be on that ship. *Any* ship. I wanted the tip and swing of the deck beneath my feet. The strong, sharp smell of tar and the gentle musk of wood. Even the cramp and the heat would be preferable to being stuck on land with a baby in my belly.

I leaned on Read as he helped me up the path and into town. Once I would have minded but now I would take any small comfort available. A storm was coming, yes, but for now the air was thick and my collar was damp with sweat. I was constantly thirsty and constantly waddling to the privy. Everything ached. The babe played merry hell with my appetite and sleep.

'Why would any woman ever go through this more than once?' I muttered between my teeth.

'Not long now,' he returned and I shot him a filthy look.

'That's not helpful.'

'What would be helpful?'

Calico. Calico would be helpful. 'I don't know.'

'Well, then.'

'Shut up, Read.'

He smiled and we walked the rest of the way to the Cunninghams'. Rose greeted us at the door, a worried frown on her freckled features. Her chubby hands were dusted with flour and there was a streak of white on her cheek. She gave Read a tight-lipped smile and closed the door in his face as soon as I was inside.

'I don't like him,' she said, just the same as she did every time. 'Jack wouldn't, either.'

'Jack's not here,' I said, as if any of us needed that reminder.

She opened her mouth, then closed it again. I didn't ask her what was on her mind. If it was important she would tell me, and if it wasn't I didn't have the patience for it. I passed her and went to my small room. It was getting harder and harder to sink down to the pallet on the floor and then pick myself up again but I wasn't going to whine. I could complain to Read all I wanted, but I wasn't going to push it too far with the Cunninghams. They were good people. They would take care of the baby, raise it proper and true—something I couldn't say for anyone else I knew. If they decided for whatever reason that they didn't want it, I didn't know where I'd turn.

'What will you do if Calico doesn't come back for you?' Rose was leaning against the doorframe, wiping her hands on her apron. She'd make a good mother, I thought. She didn't have much in common with my mother, who had been bony and sharp, but they shared the same strong will and clear eyes.

'I'll find a ship,' I shrugged.

'Without him?'

'I'm not staying on shore.' And then, because I knew it would irritate her: 'I'm sure Read could help me.'

Rose shook her head. 'I wouldn't trust him, Anne,' she said. 'He was sailing with Barnet all that time…'

'And if he'd wanted to, he could have left me *with* Barnet. Or he could have turned me in himself and demanded a reward from the governor, or from my husband, or my father, or whoever else wants me dead or captured. If Calico doesn't come back for me, I'll get Read's help and I'll be out of your hair before the baby sees its first year out.'

'I'm not trying to make you feel unwelcome.'

'Can you not-try a little harder then, please?'

I was trying not to be so vexing, but I couldn't seem to help it. The sticky heat, my stomach cramping and the baby turning inside of me. A particularly sharp wrench made me curse and reach for the wall. Rose caught my arm instead. I met her gaze. Her eyes were wide, the freckles standing out on her pale cheeks.

Another wrench and then I knew.

'Oh,' I said weakly. 'Oh, God.'

'Walter!' Rose shouted out of the room. 'Walter, go for the midwife!'

He went. Rose brought cool, fresh water and a cloth for my brow. I sank down onto the pallet and it was all so *heavy* I thought I'd never get up again. Rose crouched by me, her hands on my shoulders. I wanted to push her away but instead I leaned forward and pressed my head against her. It was hard to breathe. I was tearing apart.

Then it was just noise and blood and the stifling heat of the room, and I fell back so far into the pain and the fear and the thought of Calico that I lost all sense.

I stood at the docks, listening to the water underneath. It was black and sparkling, taking the light from ship lanterns and torches on the jetties. It was quiet here so early in the morning, before the sun could even think of rising. No sailors, no pirates, no one but me and the water.

'Where's the father?' The midwife, her hands at my shoulders, tipping something down my throat as I struggled and gagged.

'At sea.'

I had always wondered what it would be like to die at sea.

Blood and pain.

I couldn't go home. My father had disowned me. The pain from that wound was still fresh. I couldn't leave Nassau because what ship would take me? What ship would be safe? New Providence was a prison and Nassau was the oubliette, the pit, the place people went to forget and be forgotten.

Blood and pain.

I had run out of options.

Blood and pain.

Footsteps sounded along the jetty. It creaked and groaned and I was so sure my husband stood behind me. I felt like the water was rising up around my throat, even though I was still on dry ground.

'What do you want, Jim?'

'Who's Jim?'

I turned and there he was.

A long, thin cry.

'There we are,' Rose said, not talking to me or the midwife or anyone much. 'There we are, oh there you are. Little man, little man.' She was crying and for a moment I thought that was it, the baby was dead, it was over. But then the pressed wail came again and through bleary eyes I saw Rose sit and sob, a small bundle in her arms.

'He's beautiful,' she whispered. 'Oh, he's beautiful.'

'Jack,' I croaked. A sob pulled through me but I was too tired to give it voice. I tried to sit up but the midwife pushed me back down with her firm hands and I didn't have the strength to do anything about it. The baby cried and Rose cried as well. The midwife cleared up around me. She said something and pulled at the sheets around me. I felt like I was underwater, my senses blurred and thick. The baby kept crying and Rose kept saying he was beautiful. I was drenched in sweat.

'Jack,' I said again and I wasn't even sure if the sound came out.

Rose's face appeared in front of mine. Her eyes were red. 'It's a little boy,' she whispered. 'What should we call him?'

My lungs ached. 'Jack,' I said one last time. The world was thick and foggy. I had been clinging to consciousness but now it slipped away from me. I settled into an uneasy sleep with no dreams.

19

BONNY

Our baby was small and wrinkled, all red and red-headed. The hair was the only thing of mine he had inherited as far as I could tell but all babies looked much the same to me. He grizzled, grunted, made those strange little sounds that are so particular to babies. He had a good, healthy set of lungs and he used them to full effect every few hours. Had a temper, too.

He was perfect in every way, except that he was mine.

Rose and Walter were in love. They had to bring Johnny back to me to feed, at least until they found a wet-nurse, but other than that they took turns cradling him and singing to him. They called him John Arthur

Cunningham. Johnny or Jack. I didn't mind the name but it wouldn't have mattered if I'd hated it. It wasn't my decision. He was theirs now, and in just a few months I would leave their house. I would go back to the water, somehow. Even if it meant going alone.

Even as I tried to make plans without him, my mind was on Calico. I wanted him, just once, to hold his son, to see his eyes reflected back in the baby's sleepy blink. More selfishly, I wanted to hold the wretched man close and stop him from leaving me again. I got tangled in these thoughts and there wasn't much to pull me away from them.

I sat in my room one hot afternoon, sweaty and stifling, while Johnny fed. It had been a quiet, dull morning and both Rose and Walter were outside. Rose was shelling peas and Walter was gutting fish. I craved the push of the breeze but their company was stifling after so long. I was too tired and restless to go out and join them. I resolved to make myself move as soon as the afternoon rains came. I would go out and stand in the weather awhile, letting it wash out the feeling that I was being smothered.

Johnny snuffled and whined. I held him against my shoulder, readjusted my clothes, and patted him up and down the back. He obliged with a belch and I settled him in my arms once more. I knew I should take him out to Rose and Walter right away but I couldn't bring myself to stand and relinquish him. Not just at that moment.

'Don't you grow up to be a pirate,' I whispered to him. 'You keep your legs on land, right? It's much safer.' I stroked his carroty hair back with one hand.

'Don't go filling his head with nonsense, now.'

If I had been a more skittish woman I would have dropped the baby. As it was I went still, my arms tightening about him. I lifted my head.

Calico. He tried to smile, but it faltered and faded. He stepped forward, an anxious crease in his brow.

'I wanted to be here for the birth,' he said in a hushed voice. 'I wanted to be here, Annie. I'm sorry you had to be alone.'

He was thinner than I remembered. His clothes had more patches in them and he was unshaven. It looked like he had been sailing hard, living on rough waves. But his eyes were still the same, that magnificent blue, chasing any doubts I might have had. I had to remind myself of the baby in my arms. I stood, still holding Johnny close to me. I didn't know what to say.

'Calico,' I breathed at last.

He took a step closer. I reached across and grabbed his hand. It was rough and warm and I pulled him in so we were only separated by the baby between us.

'I only missed you by a day,' I said. My throat was tight and swollen and it was hard to get any words out. '*One day*, Calico.'

'Walter told me. We couldn't stay. Barnet was still hunting. His people were looking for us. We lost the *Kingston*, Annie. We lost it, and we lost you, and we couldn't take any more chances.' He touched my face. 'We didn't even know if you were alive. I came to Walter on the off-chance that you found your way here.'

I pressed a kiss to his lips. Alive. He was alive and he was *here*. He tipped his head down and leaned his brow against mine. I would have given way to tears if we stood like that a moment longer so I stepped back and cleared my throat, holding Johnny up like an offering.

'Your son,' I said.

Calico took him. He looked stiff and uncomfortable with the baby but a small smile crept across his features.

'He looks like you,' he said.

I returned the smile. 'I was going to say the same thing.'

20
BARNET

Barnet spent the better part of eight months scouring the waters for John Rackham and his crew. They always seemed to slip away from him, always seemed to be riding the crest of the next wave. But he was a patient man, and after months of waiting his patience paid off.

The *Albion* cut through the water, her bow mended and her hull careened. She was on the hunt. They had intercepted a message run by a merchant coming out of Cuba. The contents were obscure but Barnet had read the meaning well enough. The woman Bonny was still in Havana, and she was calling for her man Calico to come and claim her. Barnet had felt a moment of vicious triumph. He had no need to pursue Jack Rackham after all. He just needed to return to Havana and wait. If he had learned one thing from the woman Bonny, it was that she was adept at twisting men to her will. She had corrupted Martin Read easily enough. He did not doubt for a moment that eventually Rackham would come for her. Barnet would be waiting when that happened.

The ocean was becoming smaller for pirates; they were being harried off the waves. Once the pirates had been able to sail without fear into Charles Town, Port Royal, Nassau. Now they had to slink through the darkness, where their kind belonged. In order to catch the pirates, Barnet knew he had to occupy their minds. He was canny enough to know they would not dock in the main harbour so instead he took to the beaches, the coves, the rocky corners of the coast. Secluded bays where pirates and smugglers scurried in and out of caves with their wares.

He obscured the escutcheon of the *Albion* and took down the flags. He flew a simple black instead. It galled him to even make the pretence of piracy but he knew it was necessary. So he waited. The crew scrubbed each inch of the ship and careened her, burning off weed and prying away the barnacles. Calico Jack sailed an old ship but she was always well maintained. Barnet had each of the weapons tested. They restocked and found crewmen to replace those they had lost along the way. And they waited. Waited for the familiar sails of the *Ranger* to come in. Barnet emptied his own coffer bribing dock workers to keep him informed.

Finally it paid off. Someone sent word that the *Ranger* had been sighted to the west of Havana. She had been there for a few days.

Barnet sent men out to scout the area. They came back with information that the *Ranger* was careening… but that her captain was nowhere to be seen. Barnet gave the orders and they set out west, tacking along the coast until they caught sight of the familiar vessel. Barnet's heart sped. He gripped the rail, knuckles whitening. Even from a distance he could tell the ship was in no state to fight. There were crewmen sitting in the rigging and others out on the shore drinking. There was a good fire going on the shore and Barnet could hear the raucous shouts and laughter over the sound of the waves.

Before the pirates even realised, the *Albion* was upon them.

Barnet fired off two shots, both damaging the bow. Neither shot would sink the ship but they made the point. Reparations for the damage the *Albion* had sustained. Barnet's men armed themselves. They stormed the *Ranger*. There were only three men on board and they were drunk. The pirate hunters took the ship without resistance.

Then they went in to shore. Barnet stood on the jolly-boat, his musket pointed at the pirates. Some fought but others fled across the beach. Barnet had anticipated this. The additional men Governor Rogers had supplied came out at them from the scrub and the trees. Gunshots cracked across the still air. Three pirates fell.

'Stop!' As the jolly-boats came into shore, Barnet could hear one of the pirates bellow the order out to the others. 'Surrender!'

The pirates tried to duck around their attackers and run for the woods but they were cut off before they could reach the tree line. More fell. The governor's men herded the pirates to the edge of the water and Barnet met them there. He stepped out of the jolly-boat, into the water. He schooled his features to wipe the smile from his lips.

'Where is your captain?' he demanded.

'We killed him.' It was a slave who spoke, bold as a freeman, his eyes direct on Barnet. 'A mutiny, two weeks ago.' A skinny boy nodded his agreement.

Barnet glanced at one of his own men. 'Beat them,' he said.

The slave fought but it wasn't long before he was on his knees, then on the ground. The skinny boy folded as a man punched him in the ribs, then kicked him to the floor. He cried out, blood spurting from his nose.

Barnet kept the musket ready, his eyes sweeping across the rest of he crew. 'Shall we try again?' he asked. 'Where is your captain?'

Silence. Barnet steeled himself. He was a hunter, and pirates were his quarry. They lived in defiance of God and the law. They could die the same way. He twitched his gun to the side and shot one of the other pirates, who fell to his knees, blood flowering around the hand he pressed to his belly. Then he slumped forward into the sand, twitching. Someone let out a sharp cry. The slave stiffened, eyes wide. Barnet reloaded the musket. He did not hurry.

'This is the last time I ask,' he said. 'Where is your captain?'

The pirates looked at one another. Barnet shot another man and let the noise wash across the beach. He reloaded again and pointed the gun at the skinny boy.

'Stop. Stop!' A freckled lad stepped forward, put himself between the hunters and the other two pirates. 'Stop. He's in Havana! He went there after some girl!'

'Harwood—'

'He'll find out anyway! He'll kill us all if we don't tell!'

Barnet held up a hand and the men left the slave alone. 'Where in Havana?'

'We don't know. Somewhere near the docks. He's coming back tonight.' The freckled lad bent and helped the other young one up. Another went for the slave, stumbling under the dark man's weight. 'He'll be back tonight.'

'Then we shall wait for him.' Barnet turned to his own crew. 'Take them back to their own ship. Keep the lanterns glowing. Rackham must not suspect anything.'

'Where are you going, sir?' It was the cabin boy, Oliver, who spoke up. Stepping beyond his station. Barnet would have time to check that once this was over.

'Into Havana,' he said. 'I am taking no chances this time.' He turned to Rogers' men. 'Kill five more. Then we move out.'

The smell of blood and gunpowder filled the air.

21

BONNY

It was crowded in the house with Calico but no more so than on a ship. At night he slept with his arms wrapped around me and I rested better than I had in seven months. It was strange to play house with him. Strange and nice. I could almost forget there was a crew to consider, that there was a pirate hunter scouring the seas for us.

That this couldn't possibly last.

I walked through the house one afternoon and stopped shy of the kitchen, hearing Walter and Calico in conversation. I lingered near the door. Eavesdropping came naturally to me. In my father's household no one had told me anything, so I'd been forced to find things out on my own. It was a habit I had never bothered trying to break.

'…fiery little thing. You should have seen her the first time we had the midwife over. Your Annie chased her out before she could even lift her skirt.'

Soft laughter from Calico. 'Sounds right.'

'Poor woman was only trying to help. Will you stay? Might make things easier.'

'I can't. My ship.'

'What does Isaac have to say about all of this?' A long pause. 'You haven't told *Isaac?*'

'Still thinks she's a boy. Haven't been able to tell him. He doesn't like her much as it is.'

'I don't imagine he would. Sharp, ain't she?'

I leaned into the room. 'Careful how you answer that, Calico.'

Walter jumped, startled. 'Christ's *blood!*'

Calico just laughed. 'Aye,' he said. 'She's sharp.'

Rose jabbed me in the shoulder. 'Stop chattering and come help me,' she said. I sighed and went to her side, helping to serve out food and drinks. Calico's eyes flashed in my direction. He looked uncomfortable as I handed him the plate, and well he might. He and I could never seem to find even ground. On the ship he was the captain and the keeper of my secrets. On land, I was a woman who waited on him. It all felt wrong: jumbled and awkward.

'Sit down,' he offered, kicking out a chair for me. He was trying to be a gentleman but he didn't have the manners for it. His rough attempt made me smile, helped to ease some of the tension. Rose sat a moment later, comfortable and content beside Walter.

'When are you going?' I asked Calico. I tried to make the question casual but I could hear the edge in my own voice. Calico winced and spoke around the food in his mouth.

'Three days.'

Three days. He must have seen the expression on my face because he swallowed quickly, coughed, and added, 'Will you be ready to join us by then?'

'No,' Rose said. I opened my mouth to protest and she spoke again, stronger this time. 'No. She's still recovering, and there's no chance she can pass as a boy besides; not to mention the babe's still feeding. I'm putting my foot down here, Calico. I know you want to go together but I won't have it. You can come back for her in a month, when she's had a chance to rest.'

'I've already been resting a month,' I said. 'I'm well enough to go now.'

'Everyone in this kitchen knows that is a lie.' She folded her arms. 'You're well enough to get about but what sort of life would you lead? The work is too much for a woman not so long off the childbed. And there's plenty of things you won't be able to hide out there on the sea.'

I hated it, but she was right. I still thought I'd manage well enough with the work. I was young and strong and the birth had been successful. Women everywhere went back to work in fields and streets without the luxury of a long recovery. But hiding all the other inconvenient after-effects of pregnancy, about which no one had ever warned me, was another thing.

'We'll be back in a month then,' Calico said at length and I knew the matter was decided.

'You'll stay tonight though, won't you?' Another long pause. I felt my throat tighten. 'You're not staying tonight?'

'I can't, Annie. I have to go back to the ship.'

'Why?'

Walter cleared his throat, uncomfortable. Rose suddenly became very interested in her meal.

'I told the crew I would. I can't leave them too long, Annie, not right now. I've already spent too much time away.'

'None of *them* just gave birth to your son.' I hated that I had been backed into the role of the nag, the scold, but I felt sick with disappointment.

'I'll be back tomorrow.'

I opened my mouth to argue, to say something bitter, to try to make him stay. But instead I sat back and let my shoulders slump. Calico reached under the table and caught my hand. I forced myself to breathe and smile. This was a passing thing. In just a month I'd be back at sea. Back to Calico. I had endured Nassau for two years, and I had suffered the stifling heat of Charles Town for almost four years before that. A month was nothing at all.

I felt subdued as we finished the meal, but when it was cleared away, Walter joined Rose in the kitchen to ask her something about food for the crew. I grabbed Calico's hand and pulled him out into the cool air.

'Promise me one thing.'

He held my gaze. 'What is it?'

'This is the last time you leave me behind.'

He pressed his lips against mine. 'I promise,' he said. He hesitated. 'Annie. Sorry this is how things happened.'

I shrugged and patted the side of his face. 'For your information, Isaac adores me. He just hasn't realised yet.'

'I'm sure he'll be thrilled to see you again.'

We traded faltering smiles, both feeling the impending distance.

Calico and I walked along darkened streets, hand-in-hand: strolling like new lovers towards the docks. It was strange for us to be able to walk together in the open, without having to dodge around corners or tuck ourselves into shadows. In Nassau we had stolen moments around James Bonny's absence and every second had been steeped in fear. Onboard, I had visited Calico in the small hours of the night, heart pounding and nerves buzzing from ducking crewmen. Now, though, we took our time. For a whisper of a second I thought I could get used to this. Being…undisguised.

'You should tell Isaac,' I said at last, dropping my head against Calico's shoulder.

'Tell him what?'

'About me.'

Calico stopped walking. 'What?' he asked, a laugh shaking the word. 'Annie.'

'You should tell him.'

'You only say that because you know he'll berate me.'

'I say it because he's your friend.' I shrugged. 'Maybe he'll even like me more for it.'

'He won't.'

'At least it'll be one less person we have to lie to. The secrecy was exhausting, Calico.' I squeezed his hand. 'You trust him, don't you?'

'Of course.' He didn't hesitate, not even for a breath. I wondered what it was like to be so sure of someone.

'Well then. He won't give you away, will he? Just consider it.' I caught his questing look and tipped a shoulder. 'I don't know, Calico. These past few months have been hard but at least I don't have to bind myself down or hide my bleeding or worry about where to take a piss. I don't mind dressing as a man, living a man's life, but I hate constantly being afraid of the lads finding out. It would be easier for us if Isaac knew. He's discreet enough. I don't think he'd make it a problem.'

'I'll think about it. Maybe…' He stopped, trailing off with a frown.

'What?'

'Shh.' His hand tightened on mine. In a moment he snapped back into the role of the captain, the commander, his muscles tense and his hand on his flintlock. 'We're being followed.'

I looked down the street behind us, saw a flicker of movement some yards away.

'Do you have a spare flintlock?' I whispered.

'You can't fight—'

'I'm out of condition but I can still damn well shoot. *Do you have a spare flintlock?*'

He handed one to me. I loved the familiar weight, the cool press of the gun in my hand. I tugged Calico along, trying to act natural. Either someone was hoping to rob us or we were being hunted. We reached the end of the street and I pulled Calico around the corner. The sea was in front of us. Clouds were thick overhead, smothering the moon and the stars and whatever lights may have been flickering from the ships. Soon the rain would drive in from the water, washing across the city.

Calico would have continued down along the docks but I pulled my arm free from his and planted my feet, waiting. I readied my flintlock, ramming and wadding the weapon. It calmed me.

'Annie!'

I hissed at Calico and waited, hitch-breathed. Footsteps sounded by the corner. I didn't ask questions, I fired. There was a bang, a grunt, and someone sprawled onto the ground. I waited until he stopped moving, then stepped out and rolled him over.

I didn't recognise the man.

'Just a pickpocket,' I said. Relief made me light-headed. 'It's fine, Calico. Just a thief.'

'Are you sure?'

'I don't recognise him.' I straightened and leaned against the wall. 'Thank God. I thought we were in real trouble for a moment there.'

'Put down the gun.'

I froze. Breath snagged in my throat, I turned. Calico stood with his hands raised, his own gun on the ground in front of us.

A group of men blocked the street. Maybe five of them. Too many to shoot. Too many to fight. There was no time. They crowded forward. Someone shoved me against the wall, pinning me by my shoulders. The gun flew from my hand and skittered across the ground. I could feel a blade through my blouse, through my skirts. Pressing just enough for me to feel, without so much as slicing a thread.

'What's this?' asked the man holding the blade. He was heavy, with a beard that grew in patches and some missing teeth. 'One of your whores, Rackham?'

I met Calico's gaze. He was frozen to the spot, pinned just as I was.

'Yes,' he said at last, hoarsely, murder in his eyes. 'Just…just a whore.'

'Or is it someone special?' The man's breath was hot on my cheek. 'I hear you've been stealing women away. That you took a woman to your crew. Maybe this is her. Ugly enough to be a pirate wench.'

'She's no pirate,' Jack said. His voice was weak.

The man sneered and looked over his shoulder. 'Bring the boy.'

They hauled a child to the front, hands clamped on his arms. I recognised young Oliver right away.

Barnet had found us. Relentless bastard.

'Is that her?' the man demanded. 'Is that Bonny?'

I looked at Calico. I could speak up now. Put myself by his side. He shook his head a fraction. Wanting to keep me safe. And I knew a braver woman—a better woman—would ignore that little shake of the head and fight for him.

But if I fought for him, they would take me back to Nassau.

They would take me to my husband.

Read wouldn't be able to save me; Calico wouldn't be able to save me. I wouldn't be able to save myself.

But we'd be together.

I said nothing. Frozen.

'Nah,' Oliver said. My head jolted up. Oliver stared at his shuffling feet.

'Say again, boy?'

'Ain't her. Ain't the Bonny woman.'

I was shaking. Coward. Coward. *Coward.* But I was so afraid. My gun was on the ground and Calico was on his knees. The knife pressed a fraction closer and for a moment I thought it would cut right through, that the man was going to split me open there on the street. But he lowered the knife, thank God. He lowered the knife—

Then he hit me.

My head snapped back. I almost fell but I swung myself back up. Tiny lights flickered in front of my eyes, spinning and shining like stars off the waves. I tasted blood and spat. The men started to drag Calico away and my fear was gone like a freak wind. A flash of self-loathing hit me. *Coward.* Faithless, gutless. It was enough to strengthen me. I couldn't let them take Calico.

I ran at the man and he hit me again. My head smacked against the wall. I blinked. When I opened my eyes again I was on the ground and he was kicking me in the stomach. My body, still weak and raw from the childbed, cramped and seized. I grabbed his leg and curled around it, trying to drag him down. He bent, cracked his gun across my back, and my body spasmed. I tried to pull myself up again but he beat me down. I could hear Calico shouting, cursing. I tried to scramble to my feet. I saw him bucking and straining against the men who held him. And then he was gone around a corner, and there was a dull thud and I couldn't see him, could only hear the ocean and the receding voices of Barnet's men.

I was undone by my fear for him. That moment of pause, seeing the last of him, distracted me. The heavy man hit me. And hit me. And hit me. The world was in the wind, scattered and tossed. It was the heavy man hitting me but it was also my husband. Sedlow and his boys. Barnet. And as I curled around myself and choking on the pain, I wondered if it had always been my fate to die beneath the fist of a man.

'Virgil! Lay off, we gotta go!'

He stopped.

There was blood in my mouth. I opened my lips and let it splatter to the ground. I rolled against the wall. I tried to swim towards consciousness but all I had was James Bonny's face and my own cowardice.

Virgil spat at me. Then he laughed. His footsteps retreated.

I tried to stand. Retched. Lowered myself back to the ground and lay there, my hands in the dirt, feeling the earth tip and lean like a ship in a storm.

It was dawn before I could drag myself to my feet. By then Calico was long-gone and there was just nothing I could do except bleed and hurt and hobble back to the Cunninghams'.

I was no stranger to beatings. The first time I was thirteen or fourteen. My mother had just died and we were new in Charles Town. Most of my days in Ireland had been spent running riot, dressed as a boy, but when we arrived in America I was confined to the sticky heat of the household, wearing corsets and laces. It made me wild, and when one of the maids muttered some insult about my mother I drove a knife into her hand. My father, tolerant and distant until that point, had me whipped. It put a rift between us that never healed. I continued to push him and he continued to punish me. And once I was out of my father's household, Jim Bonny beat me at the end of his temper or at the beginning of a drinking night.

But I had never given birth before. I took a fever the night Calico was captured and that fever held me for almost a week. I remember very little: Rose's face in front of mine, Johnny's thin wail from the next room, flies buzzing around my face, the sour smell of sickness, fever dreams...

Calico was at my side, looking out at the bobbing ships. He levelled his finger towards an elderly, slim vessel to the west of the harbour.

'See her?' he asked. 'She's mine.'

She was a patchwork of different woods, a rugged

and weathered ship with keen lines. She leaned with a strong wave and then rocked back. She looked like she was beckoning.

When the fever broke I woke to a clean room and the sound of the sea outside. For a few moments I was lost in the after-breath of the delirium. I thought I could hear Calico. Felt him, close and loving and willing.

And I knew I had to go after him. To the worst place. I was sure Barnet would take him to Nassau.

'Anne.' Rose watched me as I hobbled across the room. My body felt slow, ungainly as it had when I was still pregnant. Sore. I scraped my hair back from my face and twisted it into a knot at the back of my head.

'What?'

'We can...' She hesitated. 'We can find work for you here in Havana. You can stay here until you find a place.'

I glared at her. She winced and gentled her voice.

'You know Calico wouldn't want you to lose yourself. He'd want you to go on with things. Find a life for yourself. Survive.' She reached over and touched my shoulder. 'He wouldn't want for you to put yourself in danger for him. Especially when there's nothing that can be done.'

'Have you heard any news from Nassau?'

'Nothing.'

'From Jamaica?'

'No.'

'How long has it been?'

'Over a week.'

It would only take a week to sail from Cuba to Nassau. A week to get there, a week for the news to travel back. If Barnet had reached Nassau I was sure we'd find out soon. Wanting the message to reach me—as a lesson; to reach other pirates—as a warning. We'd know within the week, but I couldn't wait that long.

'How are the seas?'

Rose paused. She held Johnny in her arms, one hand stroking absently over his tuft of orange hair. 'Rough,' she said at last. 'I heard there's storms through the north-east.'

It was a bleak time of year. Hurricanes. Waterspouts. Wrecks along every coast. 'So they might not even make it there.'

'It's possible, Anne. But there's no telling for sure. You don't even know where they went.'

'They sailed for Nassau.' When I said the words I became sure of them. Of course it was Nassau.

It had always been Nassau.

'You can't be thinking of going after him.' Her voice was sharp, eyes fixed on me.

'Calico came back for me.'

'You don't have a ship to travel with, or a crew at your back.'

'I've found both on shorter time.' *With Calico.*

'Anne.' She caught my hands. I made to pull them away but she held tight. 'Anne, stop. You are still weak. Tired. Even if you get there before he is executed, what will you do?' She reached over and touched my cheek and I thought for a moment that this must be what it was to have a sister. 'It's not our world, Anne,' she said. 'Stay here. You can watch Johnny grow up. You don't have to be his mother to see that. You can find a life here.'

I took a breath and stepped away from her.

'You're a good woman, Rose,' I said. 'And that's really the difference between the two of us.'

'I don't understand why you need to do this. Is it honour? Love?'

Honour? Love?

'No.' I set my jaw. Buried my fear. Tried not to think of Nassau. 'Neither of those things.'

Revenge.

22
BARNET

They crammed the pirates into the brig and Barnet took particular satisfaction in seeing them there, packed together, bleeding and bruised. His men, frustrated by the long hunt and their losses across the months, had beaten them savagely. Barnet had not curbed their efforts. The only one they had not been permitted to touch was the captain.

Barnet wanted that pleasure for himself.

He had Rackham brought to his cabin. The man was on his knees, dishevelled and furious. He had been spitting curses at the crew since they dragged him out of Havana but now he was silent, his jaw clenched and his eyes burning as he stared at Barnet.

Barnet allowed himself a small smile. He hunted pirates in accordance with God's will, and in retribution for the wrongs he had once suffered at a pirate's hands, but there was no harm in enjoying the work. Victory at the end of a long pursuit was a sweet matter indeed. He wondered briefly whether St George had felt this when he struck down the dragon.

'Captain Rackham.' He had his gun ready and his sword at his hip. Rackham was bound but Barnet knew better than to underestimate a pirate. They were snakes, at their most dangerous when they were desperate. 'It is a merry chase you have led us across the seas. I want to thank you for the entertainment.'

'We killed your men and blasted the *shit* out of your ship,' the pirate snarled.

'Perils of the mission,' Barnet nodded. 'Still, those men gave their lives in a noble pursuit, and have been accorded the proper honours.'

'Noble?' Rackham's face twisted. 'One of your men assaulted my woman in Havana.' There was a tight line in his voice. 'He may have killed her.'

Barnet's lips tightened. His men were fools not to have known Anne Bonny when they saw her. 'She was a pirate. Die on the street or at the end of a rope, she deserved it.'

'Bastard.'

Barnet flipped his gun and cracked the butt against Rackham's face. The man reeled, lost his balance and crumpled on the deck as a cut opened above his brow. He lay there a moment, breathing hard. Barnet reached down and pulled him upright.

'Guard your tongue, pirate,' he said. Rackham's breath shuddered. Barnet released his shoulder. 'You will no doubt be questioned when we reach Nassau, but let us make the most of the time we have on this voyage. The governor wishes to deal with your crimes, but once you are arrested and executed I still have a job to do. Pirates to pursue. So: what information have you on your brethren?'

The pirate spat at him. 'You'll have nothing from me, Barnet,' he snarled.

Barnet fished a kerchief from his pocket and wiped his face, holding at bay the fury that whipped through him. That was what the pirate wanted, after all: for Barnet to stoop to his level.

'We have a week of sailing, John Rackham,' he said, rolling the sleeves of his shirt. 'A week is a long time. By the end of it, you may be a little more willing to comply.' He stepped around the pirate and closed the door to the cabin. Rackham craned to look over his shoulder. Barnet let the gun swing again, this time cracking against his shoulder. Rackham hissed but did not cry out. Barnet leaned over and grabbed a fistful of the man's hair.

'Will you speak willingly?' he asked.

'A short life and a merry one,' the pirate snarled.

The words were nonsensical to Barnet, but the intent was clear.

Barnet smiled again. 'Very well,' he said. 'Let us begin.'

Rackham was resilient. Barnet beat him bloody that first night and still he gave nothing away. Barnet stood at the bow of the ship, eyeing the brooding sky. On reflection, he had perhaps been too enthusiastic about the interrogation. The pirate had been unable to give coherent answers by the end of it, and Barnet was forced to stop before any permanent damage was done. The governor would be displeased if he was unable to gain a proper confession. For now, Rackham had been shoved back into the brig with the rest of the captured crew. Barnet could hear them from where he stood on the deck. Sometimes they were quiet, mutters buzzing between them. Every so often, though, they broke into howls and shouts, threatening and cursing. They were no better than animals. Barnet had given the order for them to be starved for the first few days. Hopefully it would take the edge off their rebellion.

A stiff wind blew off the ocean, bringing with it the first sweep of rain. The water came on quickly, hot and heavy, and within moments it was difficult to see. Barnet closed his hands on the rail. The sails had been taken in to prevent the wind from putting strain on the mast and the hatches were battened down to prevent water from filling the lower decks. The cabin boy, Oliver, was hard at work on the bilge pump, and the other men had secured themselves to the ship with jacklines as the hard wind and waves threatened to sweep them overboard.

The crew secured themselves with jacklines and worked against the howl of the wind. They were drenched with sea-spray; the waves had been lapping at the deck for almost an hour. Jonathan was nineteen, a thin-chested boy with wiry strength. He felt that strength as he pulled ropes and climbed through the rigging. He was young enough to be reckless with the lads in port and shy of the girls who sometimes travelled on their ship. The captain's daughter, Constance, had soft brown hair. Once she dropped a kerchief and Jonathan returned it to her. The men later told him he should have kept it in his pocket, that she had intended it for him.

He taught her how to navigate by the stars.

He thought of her now as he stood on a ratline and the wind shuddered the rigging. He leaned out. He loved the ocean in all its moods but especially now, when she was brooding and bitter, snarling at those men who wished to tame her. On the starboard side, he could just make out the faint wings of another ship.

The memory hit Barnet hard in the middle of his stomach, and was gone with the next breath of wind. He stood still for a moment, gasping for air, his eyes on some remembered horizon.

Constance.

For a dizzying instant he thought he caught the scent of her perfume. Living on the ship with her father, she had worn it always. He remembered the way his heart beat double, triple, whenever it coloured the breeze. Even now the smell of lavender...

'Captain?'

The bosun, Hutchinson, wiped water out of his eyes and peered through the rain at him.

'Sir, the hatches are battened down, save for the main companionway. The sails are in. But we're looking at a mighty bad storm. Everyone's secure.'

'Very well.' Barnet drew himself upright. He was more resilient than this. He had avoided thoughts of Constance for many years. They were a distraction that brought only pain. 'Strike the royal and t'gallant yards, and the t'gallant masts. Keep Godfrey and Lane on lookout.' He wanted most of the sails reefed so the wind did not force them too hard.

The rain was coming down so hard and thick that the horizon had disappeared. The swell lifted the *Albion* slowly and then crashed her down again. The decks tilted. Barnet checked his jackline again to ensure he was steady. He had made the decision to run ahead of the storm but he was starting to doubt his judgment. Waves were starting to break over the stern. The air was thick with sea-spray. It whipped across the deck, hard and cold. There were two men on the helm, trying to keep the ship steady, but Barnet knew there was little chance of staying on course. And these waters were filled with small islands and reefs. In good weather any man with a keen eye could avoid such dangers but they were sailing blind.

A wave crashed over their stern, hitting hard on the starboard side. The ship groaned and tilted. Thunder rolled through the sky, so loud it shook the rigging. Moments later lightning cut the sky, weaving cracks in the darkness. The light echoed off the water and disappeared. The winds picked up. The *Albion* leaned hard to the portside, then righted and slipped down the side of another wave. Barnet whipped around at a shout from one of the helmsmen. The wheel had jumped out of their hands and was spinning madly. Their feet dragged on the deck as they tried to brace and bring it back under control.

Another blow to the stern. Barnet dashed the rain from his eyes. No way to tell whether they were on course now and there was no point trying to hold to it.

Barnet had to roar to be heard over the tempest. 'Sail to point!'

The helmsmen gave up trying to hold course and instead worked to keep the ship steady and upright, to prevent her from spinning like a whirligig. There was little they could do. The timbers heaved and screamed.

Lines snapped and lashed across the deck. Barnet grabbed at one of the shrouds by the mast. The vessel lurched again. A man went flying across the slick boards of the fo'c'sle; his body made a sickening crack as it hit the rail. He would have gone over but the jackline pulled taut. He dangled like a fish on the line until two men hauled him back.

'Captain!' One of the men flung open the hatch to the companionway. Water gushed down the steps.

'What are you doing?' snarled Barnet. 'Close the hatch!'

'There's no one on the pump!' the man screamed above the roar of the wind.

Barnet ran to the companionway, grappling with the knot about his waist for a moment before he was loose from his jackline. 'Bosun, close the hatch behind us.' He flung himself down the companionway. He was going to beat the cabin boy into the next month. 'Oliver!'

The boy was not waiting at the top of the pump. Perhaps something had stuck down in the bilge and he had gone to free the mechanism.

The lower decks were awash. Rats leapt across lines and beams, furred bodies flowing across the lower decks like rivulets of water. The stench of vomit was overwhelming. Barnet went down another level to the lowest deck. He could hear the pirates in the bilge, shouting and groaning. Retching. He knelt at the entrance to the bilge and called down.

'Oliver! Get up here, you lazy little swine!'

The storm was deafening. Barnet strained to hear. There was no reply from the bilge.

'Oliver!'

He squinted into the darkness of the bilge.

Saw movement there. Something bobbing.

'To me,' he said, his voice catching. He coughed. 'To me!'

A man was at his side in a moment. 'Captain?'

Barnet drew back. 'The boy's dead,' he said. The crewman startled, but Barnet did not give him time to reply. 'Remove the body. Then get two men down there to pump.'

The crewman reached down, climbing halfway into the bilge to bring out Oliver's body. The boy must have struck his head on something, down in the dark, and drowned in the rancid water. A hard twist of guilt compressed Barnet's lungs. The boy had been his responsibility; his mother…

The ship lurched again, and he turned away. There was work to do.

The storm lasted through the night. By dawn Barnet's limbs were shivering and heavy. They had lost two hands: the boy, Oliver, and the man who had been flung into the rail. He ran their deaths through his mind over and again; all the things he could have done differently. He spent a short time composing himself in his cabin before he walked out onto the deck. The crew needed to see he was in control. They were exhausted and they knew the respite would be short-lived. The waters were calm for now; the sun had clawed its way through the clouds. But already the wind was starting to lift.

'Bearing?' he murmured to Hutch as the men wrapped the bodies in canvas.

'We're off-course, sir,' Hutch replied. 'Pushing too far west.'

Barnet set his jaw. 'Repairs need to be made on the starboard rail,' he said. 'Weather-proof as much as you can and make sure the bilge pump is fully functional again. And make sure there is at least one man guarding the pirates. The last thing we need now is an escape and a mutiny.'

'Yes, sir.' But Hutch did not run to complete the tasks. There was something more important to be done first.

As they secured the canvas around the bodies with rope and weighted them with ballast-stones Barnet willed himself not to think of Constance. Not to return to a different ship, a different time, other bodies wrapped like these. He dragged himself away from the memories.

The men stood around the corpses with their heads bowed, hats in their hands. It did not seem to matter that the same men had tormented young Oliver almost ceaselessly, especially since Read's disappearance.

Barnet intoned the office of committal but there was no time for the full respects. After a few short words they tipped the bodies overboard, and when it was done the crew turned to Barnet. He felt their eyes on him.

'Back to work,' he said at last. 'We have no more than an hour before the storm hits again.' He put a hard note into his voice. 'Go!'

The men scattered. Barnet walked the length of the deck and stared out to the east. Darkness gathered, creeping towards them.

23

BONNY

The fever took a toll, but my body healed well. When I was able, I went to Read. It took me some time to find him—he'd never told me where his rooms were and he lived quietly to avoid being spotted by any of Barnet's informants. I eventually tracked him down to the docks, where I found him rolling a barrel towards a jetty. I followed him down towards the sea.

'Read.'

He caught the barrel and righted it, then turned to face me. Surprise hit his features. Then a careful blankness.

'Bonny,' he greeted. 'What happened to you?'

I drew a breath and went straight to the matter at hand. 'The *Albion* came in just over a week ago. They took Calico. They took the whole crew.' I raised my fingertips to one of the yellowing bruises on my face. 'Left me behind.'

He didn't give much of a reaction but his eyes softened. 'I'm sorry,' he said. He didn't ask about the baby. Best to leave Johnny out of things from now. Best to remind myself that he wasn't mine anymore, that he would belong to the Cunninghams from now on.

'Don't be sorry,' I said. 'They're not lost yet.'

His brow furrowed. I stepped closer to him. He had rescued me from Barnet's ship. He had brought me to Jack. We were friends, though that friendship had come quick and unexpected. I wondered how far I could push it.

'They're heading for Nassau but we might still catch them. If not, it'll still be time before a trial is held and longer still before a sentence is carried out. I have time to do something about it. So.' I wanted to sit down. The world was still unsteady and I was so tired. 'I need to get to Nassau. I need a ship.'

He sat on the barrel and started to fill his pipe. 'A ship is one thing,' he said. 'But it's no thing at all without a crew.'

'I need a ship and a crew,' I amended.

'A ship, a crew, and a plan. And rations. And charts.' He cocked his head to one side. 'Where do you expect to find these things, little fellow?'

'I was hoping you might be able to tell me.' We both knew what I was really asking. I tried for a smile. 'I suppose I'm looking for an accomplice.'

He took in a mouthful of smoke and breathed it out again. 'What makes you think I'd be so reckless? Charging with you across the ocean for folk I don't even know. Caught up in whatever danger you keep dragging along.'

My stomach sank.

'I have a job here,' he went on. 'The work's steady. The pay is reasonable. The men are decent. It's better than what I had on the *Albion* and it's better than what I had at war. Good, honest living.'

'You've had good honest living before,' I said. 'You ran an inn, you once said. Told me it wasn't the life for you.'

'I don't want to be land-bound for all of my life.' He paused there and I read into the silence: it didn't mean he wanted to join up with pirates.

My gut twisted. I could get to Nassau on my own, but I'd wanted a man at my side who I could trust. And Read was the only one besides Calico who had come even close.

'I understand.'

He winced, but I lifted a hand.

'No, it's...I understand, Read. You have something good here. And you've already done enough for me.'

'What are you going to do?'

I didn't have an answer for him. I was trying not to think about Nassau, about everything Calico was sailing towards. My silence must have been telling. Read reached over and put his hand on my shoulder.

'If I can help some other way, I will,' he said. 'But I'm not sailing to Nassau.'

Dressing as a man simply wasn't an option, not so soon after Johnny's birth. Breast-binding was painful, breeches hurt. I'd always been on the scrawny side but I'd filled out over the months. I couldn't sign on with a crew as a woman. My only option was to pay for passage to Nassau on an honest ship and hope we got there safely. I swallowed my pride and went to Walter Cunningham for the money.

He was holding Johnny. Most men left the child-rearing strictly to the women, but Walter was as besotted with the babe as Rose was. He tried to wipe his smile away when he looked up at me but I could still see it playing around his lips as Johnny yawned and slid closer towards sleep.

'Rose said you were thinking of going after them.' He shifted in his chair. 'It's folly, Anne.'

'I need to pay passage to Nassau.'

'On your own?'

'I don't have any other option.'

'No ship will take you on.'

'I can talk my way onboard.' I took a seat. I wanted to reach over and touch Johnny's face as he scrunched up his nose but it wasn't my place. I'd have to part with him for good soon, and that was as it should be. 'But I need the money, Walter, and I don't have any. Not even my pay from the jobs we did before Barnet took me. So I need to borrow from you. I'll pay it back when I can. I don't have any other assurances to give you.'

'Anne…'

'You're just going to have to take me at my word. I'm the best chance Calico has.'

'And if he's already dead?'

'Then he's dead. But what if he's not?'

Walter sighed and shook his head. I braced myself to argue, but he said, 'You don't have to borrow anything from us. Calico brought your pay when he stopped in here.'

'What?'

'And more besides. He wanted to ensure you had enough to keep you comfortable until Johnny was born, and he wanted to help us provide for the baby. I told him we did well enough for ourselves, but he insisted.' He stood and gently lifted Johnny into my arms. My son—their son—stirred and then settled. His eyes drooped and finally closed. For a moment I thought I caught a glimpse of Calico's features on his little face.

Walter rummaged around in a cupboard, then came back with a purse. He set it on the table. It was full, looked heavy.

'Good, then,' I said, not knowing how else to respond. I handed Johnny back; I tried to imagine Calico being so natural with the baby and couldn't. As for myself...well. My hands were accustomed to firearms, not infants.

'I can talk to a captain, ask him to take you on.' Walter's voice was quiet.

'Really?'

He nodded. 'Jack was always a rogue, and he spent a good portion of our younger years getting me into the worst of trouble. But then, he was always there to get me out of it again, too. And between the two of you, you have given Rose and me a great gift.' He smoothed a hand over Johnny's head. 'I know we can't stop you. If you are Calico's only hope for rescue, we want to help where we can.'

I had known Walter was a decent man but a weight slipped from my shoulders. Not just a decent man; a *good* man. I stood and kissed him on the cheek.

'When do you want to leave?' he said.

'Before the week is out. I don't—*Calico* doesn't—have time for delay.'

He nodded. 'We'll see it done.'

That evening the Cunninghams gave me paper and ink. I sat down and did something I had not done in almost four years: I wrote a letter to my father. It was not an apology. We had both come too far for such things. But I told him he was a grandfather, and that I was bound for Nassau to stand by Calico. Perhaps becoming a mother had made me sentimental, but I felt I needed to tell him goodbye.

I made my farewells to Johnny in the small of the morning. He was already awake, his eyes wide and his limbs waving as he stretched and grasped at the air. I crept into the room and took the boy into my arms, trying to memorise his face. I couldn't see anything of me there, except for that red hair.

'Stay safe,' I whispered. 'Be good.'

My throat burned and the tears were shameful, pointless, absurd, so I set him back in his crib and retreated from the room. I pulled on my boots and a loose shirt, packed one spare set of clothes. I pulled my hair back from my face and slung the bag over one shoulder. The last time I had been to sea dressed as a woman, I had been bound for Nassau as well. Eloping with James Bonny. Leaving my father and his disapproval behind in Charles Town.

The outcome would be different this time. I slipped out the door and closed it quietly behind me.

The streets of Havana were grey in the early morning, before stripes of sunlight criss-crossed the buildings and docks. The city opened up to the harbour and the sea stretched out before me, waiting for me. The sea was a dull grey, already starting to brood though the air was still. I knew from the sky we would have rough weather before the day was out. The docks were coming alive, stevedores and sailors making their way towards their ships. Some vessels were already starting to pull slowly out of the harbour, labouring before the dead wind. The keening of gulls, the crash of the ocean, steadied me.

I went down to a neat two-masted schooner that looked a nimble little thing. I was pleased; I was used to small, agile ships, and even if I couldn't work this one it was nice to know I would be treading familiar decks. She would also be fast enough for a swift passage to Nassau.

A small number of sailors stood at the jetty leading to her gangplank. I didn't have any trouble identifying the captain. There was something about the way he stood, the way the other sailors stood around him. I made my way across to them, hand tight about the strap of my bag.

'Captain O'Malley?'

The captain was a burly man with a beard that seemed to grow in every possible direction. He couldn't have been more than five years older than Calico and Walter but he looked like an old man to me. He waved his men away.

'Well now,' he said. 'You'd be Missus Bonny then.'

'Aye, sir,' I said. I'd left Ireland at thirteen but there

was still a trace of Irish in my voice and I let it come out now, thinking he might be more likely to warm to a countrywoman.

It didn't seem so. 'Cunningham told me you'd be along,' he said curtly. 'Bound for Nassau, are you?'

'That I am.'

'Without your husband?'

'I go to join him there,' I said. Walter was supposed to have handled this. *Keep it simple, Bonny.* 'My husband had to return to Nassau for business.'

'I'm not easy about you on my ship, unchaperoned. There's no other women aboard. I told Cunningham that. There a man coming with you?'

'No.'

'Then you're not coming.'

'I can pay.'

He paused. I could see him wavering. I ground my teeth, frustrated and angry. I had sailed for months and I could shoot better than almost any man I knew. I had killed men. I wasn't going to turn back now.

'I can pay,' I repeated, trying to keep my temper under control. 'And...'

'Annie!'

I jumped as an arm came across my shoulders. I would have spun, shrugged the arm off, given someone a good punch to the face, but I realised halfway through turning that it was Read standing beside me. I froze.

'Sorry I'm late.' He extended a hand to the captain. 'Martin Read.'

The captain didn't move. 'And who's that when he's home?'

'Missus Bonny's cousin.' He caught his breath. 'I just came from the other side of Havana. We had thought I wouldn't make it in time. I'm here to chaperone Anne to Nassau.'

I stared at him. He sported a black eye and his shirt was rumpled. Something had stirred his usual calm and though he lied easily enough I could tell something was wrong. He was spooked, or hurt, or…I couldn't put my finger on it.

Captain O'Malley looked at me.

I leaned against Read, smiling at him to hide my surprise, my pure relief. 'Just like you to be late, Cousin Martin.'

'You both look like you've been brawling!'

We waited.

'Do you have passage enough for you both?'

'We can manage,' I said before Read could answer. I had just enough to get us both there. Nothing for any passage back.

Read's arm tightened on my shoulders as we waited for the captain to give us his reply. He hesitated but the crew was working around him and several of the men looked like they needed his attention. Finally he relented.

'Fine,' he snapped at last. 'Go on aboard. But mind you stay out of the way when the crew is working, Missus Bonny. A ship is no place for a woman to be meddling.'

Read and I walked up the gangplank arm in arm. I leaned in.

'What changed your mind?' I asked. 'You look terrible. What happened?'

He glanced at me out of the corner of his eye. 'Didn't you hear the captain?' he said. 'A ship is no place for a woman to be meddling. Someone clearly needs to keep an eye on you.'

I opened my mouth to press him but I saw the expression on his face. There was a shadow there, a ghost of fear. I had never seen it in him before. And I didn't ask what had driven Martin Read away from Havana, when only a week before he had been so determined to stay.

24
BARNET

The storms grew in the south-east and pushed north-west, harrying the *Albion* further off-course. After the first few weeks of gruelling sail they glimpsed the coast of Florida. They were low on supplies by then, and the constant heave and turn of the ship affected even the hardened sailors, including Barnet himself. And while the open decks were battered with wind and rain, the conditions below decks were dire in a different fashion. Illness swept the ship, starting with the pirates and spreading to the crew.

Barnet passed through the orlop deck and neared the brig. His stomach turned at the stench. The pirates were in a bad way. One of the younger men, James Dobbin, who had taken worse than the others, was huddled in a corner, shivering and occasionally bending over to retch. Noah Harwood, roughly the same age, sat with him, talking low. He stopped when Barnet neared and shook awake the tall slave they called Isaac. Soon all the pirates were awake. Some were too ill to pay Barnet much mind but the others watched him warily.

John Rackham's bruises were an ugly yellow but his eyes were bright when he lifted his head. He struggled to his feet, stooping under the ceiling, and wrapped his fingers around the bars.

'Barnet,' he rasped. 'I must say, I don't think much of this voyage. We'll be glad to reach Nassau, nooses be damned.'

'You are flippant for a doomed man.'

'You are sure of yourself for a lost man.' Rackham bared his teeth in a smile. 'A little off-course, aren't we? I heard one of the men saying they sighted the Keys.' He clicked his tongue.

'Do not attempt to rile me, pirate,' Barnet spat.

'We need fresh water.'

'You will have what I give you.' He had planned to bring fresh water down for the pirates but he had no intention of letting Rackham think he was in a position to give orders. 'And you will wait for it.'

'How many men have you lost so far, Barnet?'

The words stopped Barnet in his tracks. They prickled at him. There was a warmth in Rackham's voice that he did not like.

'Each crew has a breaking point,' the pirate went on. 'I sailed under Charles Vane for a while, you know. I was his quartermaster. And a more loyal crew you'd never see. That is—until he lost his nerve. As soon as he started abandoning ripe prizes, their loyalty snapped like a thin rope.'

'Hold your tongue.'

'How far do you think you can push your men? Have they seen conditions this bad before?' Rackham smiled. 'Perhaps by the end of this voyage we'll have a whole ship full of pirates. Most men have a price. Maybe they'll take the promise of riches and revenge on you. I am sure we can offer more hope than you can.'

Barnet returned to the bars. He kept his voice low and steady.

'If I suspect you are attempting to corrupt my crew, I will dispose of the rest of yours. I will leave only you alive, Rackham. And after you are finally dragged through the streets of Nassau, you will be tried alone and you will hang alone. Do not test me. I am a man of my word.'

Rackham opened his mouth but the tall slave touched his shoulder. The younger pirate, Dobbin, retched again.

'Captain.' The bearded pirate quartermaster, Richard Corner, spoke from where he crouched by the old slave.

Rackham glanced back at them. His jaw was locked. Hatred burned in his eyes but eventually he stepped back from the bars.

'Watch your back, Barnet,' he hissed. 'There won't always be bars between us.'

The pirate was a prisoner. Beaten down, sick, crammed in with the tattered remains of his crew. Unarmed, half-starved, thrown around by the storm like die in a cup. Even so, his stare slipped past the wax seal Barnet had put on his nerves and for a moment the pirate hunter was uneasy.

He turned on his heel and retreated to the upper decks.

25
BONNY

Because I was paying enough, I had a cabin. It was one of the only three on the ship, the others belonging to the captain and the quartermaster. I found myself searching for traces of tobacco or brandy in the air. Instead, the smell of spices stored in the orlop drifted through the entire ship.

Read and I alternated between resting on the bunk and the floor of the cabin with a few sacks and blankets for comfort. Read, never exactly verbose, was unusually subdued. By the end of the first day his silence was putting me on edge.

'Tell me about the war,' I said.

'What about it?'

'Everything. How many men have you killed?'

'Have you always been such a ghoul?'

'Without a doubt. How many?'

He shrugged, sitting back against the wall of the cabin. He bit into a strip of dried beef and thought for a while.

'Hard to say,' he mused eventually. 'I cut down a lot of men, but I didn't stop to check their vitals. Some may have survived. You don't think about it so much, in the heat of it all. It's different at sea. More contained. Out on the fields...' His eyes drifted to some far-off place.

'Well?'

'It's a different world.'

'I wish I could go to war.'

'No. You don't.' He handed me some of the jerky. 'If you must take up a sword, Bonny, stay at sea.' We ate in silence for a while before he surprised me by pressing the conversation on. 'What about you? I expect you've been counting.'

'Three or four. Mostly among the crew of the *Albion*, to be honest.'

'And before you came to sea? Any land-bound murders?'

I hesitated, thinking beyond Nassau, back to Charles Town where I had spent much of my life. I had seen slaves walking with blood staining through their shirts.

Had heard stories of monstrous cruelty from men who washed up and sat at dinner with us after church on Sunday. I glanced at Read. Cleared my throat. 'I stabbed a maid when I was fourteen. One of the women who came over to Charles Town from Ireland with us. She insulted my mother.'

Read stared at me. 'Did the maid die?'

'No. Knife went into her hand but it didn't cut all the way through, and it was a clean wound.'

'What happened then?'

'My father paid her for her silence.' Read waited, listening. I found myself going on. 'Two years after that, just before I met my husband, one of my father's men tried to...he put his hands all over me.' I could remember the way I shook, the rage igniting me like a linstock. But I had known greater pains and worse indignities since then. Now all I could feel was a dull pang of shame at the memory. I realised, vaguely, that I had never told this story before. Not even to Calico.

'What did you do?'

'I took up a poker and beat him until he couldn't stand.'

'Good.'

We traded grim smiles.

'Tell me about your life at the inn,' I said eventually. I nudged Read with my foot when he didn't answer. 'Come on. I've been entirely too frank with you, and you haven't given me a single full answer.' I grinned. 'Did you have a sweetheart?'

Read's smile was gone. Finally he jerked his head in a nod. 'I did.'

There was something constrained and pained in his voice. I should have known to let things be, but: 'What happened?' I pressed.

I saw the grief stoop his shoulders and tighten the lines of his face. He turned his eyes away and said nothing. I opened my mouth to break the silence, to apologise, to say *anything* to wipe that haunted look off his face. But eventually he spoke.

'Measles,' he said. 'Got into the lungs.'

A long, hard death. 'I'm sorry.' I wasn't used to speaking the words but they had never come so readily from my lips.

He lifted a shoulder. We sat in gentle quiet, listening to the waves on the hull and the dull sounds of sailors moving on the upper decks.

'How did you meet Rackham?' he asked at length.

'Nassau.' I scraped a hand through my hair. 'He'd taken the King's pardon and was planning to sign on with a merchant ship, him and the others. Then he met me. He tried to bribe my husband into giving me up but the governor intervened. I told Calico the only way we could be together was on his ship. I never expected him to even consider it.' A smile found my lips, in spite of me. 'But he didn't hesitate.'

'What are you going to do when we get to Nassau, Bonny?'

He was sitting straight now and I knew he had been waiting for a chance to bring the conversation here.

'I'm going to rescue Calico.'

'I see.' He didn't sound convinced. 'And what will you do if the worst has happened? What if he's dead?'

'I'll burn Nassau to the ground. Starting with Jonathan Barnet.'

I couldn't spend too much time on the open decks. I didn't want to push my luck with the captain. So for the most part I stayed in my cabin. It was better than travelling in the brig but confinement made me edgy. I paced the length of the cabin, wishing I could stop thinking about Calico, wishing I could just go outside and shoot something.

Read was a patient man but it only went so far. At the end of the third day he walked out of the cabin and spent a few hours on the deck, presumably just to get away from my restless energy.

I flopped onto the bunk and worried at my hair. What if Calico *was* dead? The thought rattled around in my skull, echoing until my head pounded. He could be drowned. Beaten to death. Hanged. Hanged. Hanged and tarred and strung up.

'Bonny.'

I hadn't even seen Read come back in. He threw a waterskin at me and it landed on my stomach.

I sat up. 'What?'

'Get up.' He rolled up his sleeves.

Wariness flickered through me. 'Why?'

'I've seen you shoot, so I don't imagine that needs much work. How are you without a gun?'

'I get by.'

'You've spent eight months carrying a child and another few months recovering. Done any fighting during that time?'

'I shot someone in an alleyway, but that's about it.'

A fleeting smile shot across his face. 'Come on, then. I think we could both do with a little practice.'

My body was still soft from childbirth. I'd lost my milk during the fever but my breasts were still sore. All the same, I wanted to see Read fight. He was tall and broad-shouldered and I didn't doubt that he knew how to use the muscle he had. This was a man who had seen war.

'Not much room in here, is there?'

'We'll make do.' He was relaxed and easy. There was a gleam in his eyes and once again I felt a thread of kinship. I bounced to my feet and rolled up my own sleeves.

'I'll do my best not to hurt you,' I told him and he snorted. Then his smile was gone and he circled me. He moved with a prowling grace, comfortable in his skin.

'Going to fight, Read, or just stand there?'

Then I was on my back, gasping for air and blinking in surprise at the speed of the blow.

Read offered me his hand and I slapped it away, irritated. I rolled to my feet and bounced on my heels, trying to regain myself. The next blow came from the left. I didn't even have time to fall before he hit me from the right. My torso swung and I almost lost my feet again. I pushed off the wall of the cabin.

'Not holding back, are you?'

Read watched me coolly. He didn't even look flushed. He wasn't using a tenth of his strength and he was knocking me senseless. I swore at him and lunged. He thrust the flat of his forearm into my belly and grabbed the back of my shirt, flipping me over his arm and back to the floor. My feet hit the ceiling before I fell. I grabbed for his shins. He stopped shy of stamping on my fingers, but he swept my hands away.

Read offered his hand again. This time I grabbed it and bit down hard. Read yelped. I clamped my teeth until I tasted blood. The tall man grabbed me by the scruff of my neck and yanked me to my feet, then held me against the wall of the cabin. He wasn't hurting me but there was no way I could get out of his grip. I spat and wiped my mouth.

'You taste like shit and you fight like a child,' I said, half-joking and half-trying to provoke him.

'You let your temper control you, little fellow,' he replied. 'You talk when you should spare your breath. You don't *watch* your opponent. You don't take your time, and you don't use your size to your advantage.'

'Piss off,' I snapped, suddenly at the end of my tolerance. I made for the cabin door, seething. I'd expected a friendly sparring match, not to have my arse handed to me.

'Don't get angry at me, Bonny. I may not hold back, but I won't kill you. Barnet will. So will anyone else you go for.' He wiped his hand on his breeches. 'Try again.'

I stopped at the door. He was right. Barnet wouldn't make the same mistake twice, even if I *was* a woman. And we were headed for Nassau. What if we came across James Bonny? I needed to be able to defend myself. I'd survived on luck and cunning with Sedlow, and with a marksman's aim in battle, but if it came to unarmed combat I'd lose. I knew I'd lose. Maybe Read was right. Maybe anger wouldn't always carry me through. I wiped my mouth and turned back to him.

'Don't just hit me,' I said. '*Teach* me.'

'Very well. You have some bad habits to break.' I opened my mouth to argue and he held up a hand. 'We're going to be here for hours if you argue with every single thing I say. That's the *first* bad habit.'

I smirked. 'Fine.'

'Now. Do as I do.'

What followed was a series of slow drills, building strength and predicting an opponent's next moves. Read was steady and patient. At one point I made him explain something to me seven times, just to see how long it would be before he snapped and lost his temper. Even then, all he did was cock an eyebrow at me and ask me to bring my mind back to task. By the time the bell rang for the evening meal I was sore and exhausted.

Read wasn't even sweating.

My body was still recovering from the trauma of the birth and I couldn't spar with Read for long periods of time. Every so often I left the cabin to get fresh air. One afternoon I even swung myself down into the netting below the bowsprit, sitting there just beneath the prow and enjoying the cold waves as they reached up to greet me. The air was still hot and sticky so it was a relief to be out in the sea-spray, away from the stifle and stench of the lower decks. When I closed my eyes I could almost imagine I was back on the *Ranger* with Isaac at the helm and Calico waiting for me in his cabin. It was a nice dream, even if it only lasted a few moments.

The captain's voice put an end to it.

'What are you doing down there?' he snarled, poking his head over the bow. 'Get back up here, you silly little chit.'

I bit back a reply. It was always prudent to stay in the captain's good graces. Reluctantly, I hauled myself up to the decks and stood quiet as the captain berated me. I let it roll off my back, making myself think of Calico. It would all be worth it if we could get Calico back alive. When the captain sent me below, I went without protest. My stomach was hot with anger and my fists were clenched but I held my tongue.

'Read,' I said as I pushed open the cabin door. 'The captain of this ship is a bastardly…'

I stopped.

Read whipped around in the midst of changing, face taut, and grabbed for the shirt lying on the bed.

'Knock!' he snarled, angrier than I had ever seen him. Panic made his voice thin, raw. He pulled the shirt on but it was too late. I'd already seen the strips of cloth wrapped about his chest. Breast-bindings. Almost identical to my own.

I pulled the door closed behind me. Read stood with his fists clenched, his eyes burning into me. I recognised his posture from our sparring. I knew how close he was to hitting me.

'Read.' I lifted my hands and stepped back. 'Peace.'

'Peace?' He looked torn between belting me across the face and breaking down in tears.

'I don't understand. What do you think I'm going to do?' He didn't say anything so I went on. 'Look, you don't have to tell me anything, God knows I owe you enough, but I'm not laughing and I'm not passing judgment.'

Slowly, my hands still lifted so he could see them, I sat on the cot. I kept my eyes on Read. The anger seemed to leach from him. His fists unclenched and after a moment he began to lace his shirt. His fingers were shaking.

'You should have knocked,' he muttered.

'I should have. I'm sorry.'

More than anything this seemed to bring him ease. His shoulders loosened.

'You weren't to know,' he said grudgingly.

'I still don't,' I pointed out. He tensed again and I rushed on. 'And I don't need to. You don't have to explain anything to me, Read. You've saved my arse more than once. I owe you my life: I can give you privacy when you want it. But...' I shrugged. 'You know my secrets. You've never treated me different because of them. Don't see any reason it should change when it's the other way around.'

Silence settled between us. Read knotted his hands behind his neck and stood staring at me, his dark eyes intent.

'You don't take anything seriously,' he said at last.

'Read. You've seen me half-drowned, imprisoned, terrified. Pregnant. It's not as if I have any ground above you.'

Miraculously, that was enough to make him smile. 'True.'

'Is it fair to say my life and trust have been almost completely in your hands since the moment you scooped me out of the ocean?'

'I'd say so.'

'Well, then. Give me the benefit of the doubt. If you want to.'

He sat down beside me on the cot. His face was still guarded, wary.

'I don't talk about this,' he said. 'I never talk about this. Most of the time, it isn't safe. It could get me hanged.' I nodded. He breathed hard a second, as if he was about to fling himself into cold water. When he spoke the words came out quickly, as if he had to rattle them out with momentum or he would never reach the end of the sentence. 'When I was born the midwife pronounced me a girl. My mother called me Mary.'

I opened my mouth, then shut it again. I didn't know what to say.

'I told her my name was Martin when I was about five. It took some…stubbornness, but eventually she accepted it.' His lips quirked. 'She was more amenable when she realised there was an elderly relative I could inherit from as a boy, but not as a girl. From then she didn't mind. She shut her mouth. Let me go to sea. Let me go to war.'

'And…' I watched Read. His narrow features and searching eyes. 'And your sweetheart?'

His smile was bitter. *Measles,* I remembered him saying. *Got into the lungs.*

'His name was Henri,' he said. 'We were in the same regiment. When the war ended I dressed as a woman so we could run the inn together without…'

Without suspicion. Without being attacked. Without being arrested. Sodomy was a hanging offence. Two men running an inn together was no strange thing, but I knew from experience how hard it could be to keep intimacy secret. And in a small community, full of God-fearing folk, the smallest glance or brush of fingers could mean ruin. I nodded, my stomach twisting. I had lived a lie for just a few months and it had worn me down. I wondered how long Read and Henri had been forced to keep their secret. How long Read had pretended to be a happy wife.

Read cleared his throat. 'When Henri died there was no reason for me to stay, or to keep being Mary. So I came back to sea. Back to who I am.'

Martin Read. Martin Read, who bound his breasts just as I did, and had to deal with bleeding every month, just as I did. Except for him, living as a man was the truth. I could read it in his face, hear it in his voice. I'd never doubted him.

'In Cuba. Your bruises…'

'The other stevedores.' He lifted a shoulder. 'They called me a sodomite. I don't think they really guessed about me, but it was a matter of time before they did.

I had to get out first. It's always been this way, every crew, every work detail. I never stay more than a few months at a time.'

'That's hard.'

'It's life.'

And that was it, I realised. The reason Read had helped me on Barnet's ship, the reason he had come after me now. Though our situations were different in many ways, we both had things to hide. And perhaps he had realised somehow, that I could be trusted. He'd seen a kinship in me, the same kinship that had made me trust him.

He paused and cleared his throat. Squared his shoulders, waiting for some sort of blow. 'I imagine you have questions.'

I did. I wanted to know if he hated the discomfort and secrecy of breast-binding as much as I did. I wanted to know how he hid his monthly courses. I wanted to know if he was glad to share his secret—if it was a relief or just another burden. I had a hundred questions and they occurred to me one after another, buzzing around my head. But when I looked at his face, the careful stillness of his features, the noise died and left just one. The rest could come later, if he wanted to tell me.

'One thing.'

'Well?'

'What name do I call you?'

His face tightened with surprise. 'What?'

'Do I still call you Read? Or...Mary, or Martin?'

It was a while before he responded. I couldn't for the life of me guess what was happening behind those eyes of his. Then he nodded. 'Read,' he said. 'You still call me Read.'

'Good. You still call me Bonny. I'll still call you Read. You save my arse, I'll save yours one day. Nothing changes, except that we know each other a little better now.'

I saw relief flash through his eyes. Relief, and surprise, and something that looked like exhaustion. I touched his shoulder. We sat for a while without talking. There was still a flicker of tension between us, an uncertainty.

'Rum?' I said at last.

'Yes,' he said, his reply so quick that we both started laughing. I got up and went off to the lower decks, searching for some rum to steal.

Several days later I walked through the ship, trying to ease the knots out of my sore muscles. They were the good kind of sore; stiff and hindering, but signifying hard work well-done. Read was a good teacher. He knew there was only so much we could achieve in half a week so, for the most part, we focused on tricks and ploys, ways to get the best out of my size and strength, how to adapt to different environments. We sparred through the rough weather, through the storms and rain that shook the little schooner. It helped to take my mind off the familiar islands I could make out from the upper decks. The reefs and coves I knew so well. The quiet closeness of Nassau.

I was desperate for some sort of real plan but there was no way to move forward until we reached New Providence Island. We were still a few days out.

Voices came from around the corner. I drew back into the shadows of the orlop, not in the mood to talk to anyone. I was restless and I just wanted to walk the ship a few lengths, stretching my legs.

When the captain walked by I was glad of my decision. I didn't have the energy for his disapproval.

'Send word as soon as we dock,' he was saying quietly to one of his men. 'Run ahead. I want soldiers on the jetty before she has a chance to escape. They say she's a slippery one.'

'Aye, sir. I'll wake Warnes and Barkley. Those two can handle anyone.'

I held my breath and let them walk on as the fear hit me, jolts that landed in my chest, in my throat, in my skull. They must have been Barnet's paid informants. Must have known from the beginning who I was, who Read was. A hundred options flew through my mind. I could get my gun, kill the captain. The crew would kill me on the spot or overwhelm me and lock me in the brig.

I'd be no better than when I was Barnet's captive. Even worse, Read would be lumped in with me. We could repeat our escape in Cuba, slipping away on a jolly-boat—except that they intended to lock us in before we dropped anchor, and that just left us too exposed, especially as the day was still young.

I turned on my heel and dashed back to our cabin, my heart setting a wild pace against my ribs. I had to warn Read. I hammered on the door and then skidded through it without waiting for a response. Read looked up from where he had been mending his boot, a frown crossing his features.

'We've been betrayed.'

He froze.

'Read, we have to get off this ship. The captain's planning to sell us out. They're going to lock us in and soldiers are meeting us at the docks.'

'Are you a strong swimmer?'

'Yes.' Much to my father's dismay I'd spent a lot of my childhood ducking and diving into ponds and lakes—and the ocean, when it was handy. 'But I don't know if that'll be enough.'

'There are plenty of islands nearby...'

'There's a difference between a sailing distance and a swimming distance, Read. I don't know if either of us will be able to make it that far.'

'We might not have a choice.'

We both fell into a tense silence. His lips moved without sound and I knew he was going through different options in his mind. I fidgeted and shifted, wanting to pace, to shout, to talk it through. I wanted Calico, the bold captain. I wanted his flare and fire.

'Fire.'

Read's head jerked up. 'What?'

'Fire. We have to set the ship on fire.'

'You're mad.' He kept his voice low. 'We can't set the ship on fire, Bonny.'

'It's made of wood.'

'You know what I mean.'

'We wait until we're about to drop anchor. Then, while they're fighting the fire, we swim for shore. We'll be close enough in to make it, and besides anything the water's shallow in these parts and there are reefs and sandbars we can walk over.'

'But…' Again he stopped and I watched his mouth move as he weighed it.

'It's the best chance we have,' I said.

He paused, then gave a curt nod. 'It'll do. I'll set the fire. They won't care much about me: you're the target. I won't rouse as much suspicion if anyone sees me out and about with the cargo.'

'I'll come with you.'

'No,' he said, and his voice was sharp. 'No, you need to stay here. Make up a bed to look like I'm sleeping.'

'I'm not staying here so they can lock me *in*, Read.'

'You have to.' He was already at the door.

'Read—'

'No. Listen, listen. If they think we're in the cabin, they'll let down their guard. If they have to hunt for you, they'll find me lighting the fire, or they'll corner you and use violence to apprehend you. But if you stay in the cabin they'll just lock you in. Once I set the fire, they'll be so busy dealing with it I'll be able to free you.' He caught my hesitation and reached for my hand, gripping around my thumb. 'Bonny, you're going to have to trust me.'

If I could trust anyone, it was Read.

'They'll have a barrel of powder,' I said. My voice was thick and it hitched. I cleared my throat. It wouldn't do for him to think I was afraid. 'They only have one gun so it won't be large, but it'll still tear a hole in the deck and maybe even the hull if the fire gets to it. Start the fire at the bow so we have time to get away. Take my gun. Just in case.'

'But—'

'They want me alive and you're my best chance of that.' I grinned. '*Again;* you're getting into a bad habit of saving me. Take the gun. If you die I'm lost anyhow, probably.' My breath was shallow. I tried to keep my voice strong. 'I'm not going to Woodes Rogers. I'm not going back to my husband.'

He took my flintlock and stared at me for a moment, searching my face.

'Don't get us killed,' I said.

'I'll do what I can,' he said, and was gone.

26
BONNY

I was sitting so quiet and still in the cabin, I heard it when someone slid the bolt across. My stomach knotted. I was trapped inside.

Moments later there was the unmistakable groan of the anchor lowering into the water, the pull against it as the ship came to a stop. Somewhere aboard, Read was carrying both our fates on his shoulders. I didn't have much time to digest all he had told me but it was enough simply to know that he trusted me. That I could trust him. And after all, his way of living was not so very strange to me. We both went through the same motions, the same secrets. We just felt differently about it. I shook my head. When I was a child my father had dressed me as a boy as part of an inheritance scheme. Read and I even had that in common.

I had to trust him.

Footsteps outside the door, the faint click and whisper of a flintlock being rammed and primed. They were standing guard. I had to remind myself this was part of the plan. Read would set the fire and they would be distracted. Even the most loyal crewmen knew to save their own skin when it came to fire on a wooden ship. Then he would come back and unlock the door, let me out.

Murmurs outside. From the cabin I couldn't hear sounds from the dock but I knew we were within swimming distance: the ship was small enough even to cross the shallow waters of Nassau's harbour. We would have to swim in the shadow of the other ships, then hide beneath a jetty until we had a moment to break across the docks and into the town. There were plenty of places to hide in Nassau. Governor Rogers was doing his best to stamp the lawlessness out of the town but pirates had a tight hold there and pirates made room for their own. Someone would take us in. We'd find a place to hide until we could get word of Calico. And then we would find a way to get him back.

It was hard to keep still. Hard not to pace or make a sound. What was taking Read so long? Maybe the fire was already lit but no one had noticed. Maybe he'd been discovered; dragged to the upper decks, beaten, thrown overboard.

My hands were white-knuckled on my knees. Any moment now. Any moment and I would hear a clamour, shouting. I would smell the smoke. Read would come to the door. We would escape into Nassau.

Nassau.

Don't think about Nassau.

Where the hell was Read?

I held off. Clung to hope. Sat staring at the door, willing tendrils of smoke to curl beneath it. For screams and shouts to fill the ship. For Read to appear.

Nothing.

I stood slowly, my fingers wrapped around a belaying pin Read had smuggled in. I should have taken my chances earlier, risked the swim. I should have kept my gun. *God* I should have kept my gun. I had thought I was clever, planning ahead, trying to step faster than the men pursuing us. *Do you ever stop scheming?* I could hear heavier footsteps now, the rattle and clank of weaponry. Men speaking in curt, abrupt voices. My own mistakes battered my mind. Fear made my skin slick. Read's lessons would do me no good. The belaying pin would do me no good.

Where was Read?

The door slammed open. I was on my feet. I swung the belaying pin, hit a man in the face. He reeled back.

I used the wall of the cabin, kicked out at another man. He doubled over his stomach with a grunt. The belaying pin spun in my hand and I turned to hit a third.

Stopped dead.

A gun jabbed into my stomach.

Panting, I looked up. Weighed my options. *What did I have? What could I use?*

Nothing. Panic hit me like a hard wind against a sail. There was always something but now, here, I couldn't think of a way to save my own skin.

'Put the weapon down.'

Except surrender.

I dropped the belaying pin and it clattered to the ground. A man grabbed me by my hair, yanked my head back. I tried to keep my footing but they kicked my legs from under me. The jolt ripped out some of my hair. I hissed. They wrenched my arms behind my back. I felt my shoulder lock and strain, thought for a moment they would pop it right out of the socket. They tied my hands tight, and someone belted me across the face. Dragged me up by the hair as I fell, spitting the blood that filled my mouth. Hard to see straight. I was on my feet but barely. They shoved me out of the cabin and through the ship. I saw the captain, O'Malley, take a pouch of money from one of the men. I wanted to howl at him, to scream and fight and curse, but I couldn't find my voice. I let them drag me up the companionway and into the fresh air. My eyes swept the deck for Read. Dead or captured? *Dead or captured?* I couldn't see him anywhere.

I tried to find my feet but they moved quickly and I stumbled as we came to the gangplank. When I righted myself I looked straight into the port I had spent so many months avoiding.

Nassau.

I could smell it from the ship.

The flat, heavy reek of shit and brine. Rotten fish and conch-flesh. Animals too, though they were a quiet note in the symphony of stench. The sands of New Providence and the surrounding islands were white and the water was impossibly blue but the town of Nassau itself was a brown smudge on the land. There was a fort, that was where Governor Rogers had staked his claim on the town, but most of the buildings were run-down timber shacks. The streets were a mixture of dirt and dung. When I first arrived there, just sixteen, there had been plenty of blood in those streets.

Clinging to the town, like the taint of shit and sea-waste, was the memory of James Bonny.

The soldiers shepherded me down the gangway. My limbs were heavy and weak, my face throbbing and swollen. I breathed in the sour air and almost threw up.

It looked like Nassau had cleaned itself up since the arrival of the new governor, though. People walked the streets with families. Respectable people, even. Nassau, like Charles Town before it, was becoming part of the New World. Apart from that stink.

The guards dragged me along the docks. A familiar ship caught my eye: the *Jeremiah and Anne,* darling Darling's ship, was tucked into a quiet mooring. The sight gave me a flicker of comfort: still a pirate's town.

Fishermen paused and straightened, watching as the soldiers marched me towards the fort. It was a four-pointed grey stone building at the west end of the port. The walls rose higher on the northern side, facing out to the harbour. The fort was in a bad place strategically but in that moment, towering, it carried the promise of the gallows.

I had walked this road once before, brought before Governor Rogers on charges of adultery. He was new to the post then, striding into Nassau like a middle-aged avenging angel. He told me to return to my husband and submit to him on pain of public flogging. I sailed away with Jack that same night.

Now I tried to stop at the entrance to the fort. My feet dug into the ground, my breath came tight and shallow. I was afraid of being convicted, afraid of being hanged, but more than anything I was afraid they would give me back to my husband. I would rather dance the hempen jig, as pirates said, than die at his hands in the dark shack where I had been a prisoner for two long years.

The soldiers pushed me forward. I felt the musket at the small of my back.

Woodes Rogers came to greet us at the entrance. Roughly forty years of age, a seaman born and bred, he carried himself with upright military bearing. His hands were folded behind his back, his shoulders square. His clothes were so stiff they hardly moved when he sighed.

The flesh around his eyes was grey. His lips were dry and cracked. His vice-like grip on Nassau was costing him his health.

'Mistress Bonny,' he said. 'I had hoped I would not see you in these circumstances a second time.'

I mustered a shrug and tried to keep my voice light. 'What can I say? I live to disappoint.'

'Flippancy ill becomes you, madam.' Woodes Rogers had been a fierce commander cross-decks and I could see it in him now. His crew would have stepped-to smartly when he gave an order—nothing like our ragged band of cut-throats. 'I think you underestimate the gravity of your situation.'

'Then you're mistaken,' I said. If I kept my tone brash, forced a swagger into each shuffling step, perhaps I could feel braver. It had worked before. 'I walk with my eyes open, Governor Rogers. Where's Barnet? Where's my Calico?'

His brows drew together and he turned to the guards escorting me. 'Bring her inside,' he said.

The fort had been a dilapidated old pile when I arrived in Nassau three or so years before. Years under pirate rule meant the buildings were neglected in favour of the ships and when Rogers arrived, I'd heard, there was just the one gun in the fort. He had made some improvements since then but the fort was still in dire need of work. The bricks were crumbling and moss-licked and the open ground was rough, uneven beneath my feet. I breathed in the scent of wood and tar and smoke. Men-at-arms trained in the yard but they were really no more than boys-at-arms. Most of them looked younger than Dobbin and Harwood. Lads who had come out here to Nassau because they were too naive—stupid—to know what sort of shit they were being shovelled into. Rogers had brought Nassau quickly into line but I imagined the initial victories were souring, proving less complete than he had hoped.

Rogers led us into a small chamber with a heavy door. Not a cell but an office of sorts. There was a stout table and wooden chairs. I dropped into a chair before it could be offered to me. One of the soldiers jerked me up by my shoulder and I laughed at how petty that was when they shoved me back down again as soon as Woodes Rogers took his seat.

'Adultery is one thing. Piracy is another.'

He wasted no time. I couldn't help but admire that about him. Rogers was a hard man—he'd had to be, to survive two years in Nassau and actually bring it to some good. If I had been a man, or at any rate an obedient one, I could see myself serving under him.

There was some commotion outside. Rogers' eyes flicked to the door, distracted, and then he looked back at me.

'I am loath to condemn a woman to the noose,' he said. 'And if you see trial, madam, you will certainly be condemned. Do you understand that?'

More noise from outside, and then the door jerked open. One of the guards peered in, looking sheepish.

'Governor Rogers, sir,' he said. 'Some lawyer fellow. Says he's here representing the interests of a William Cormac?'

I sat up. Clenched my fists and tried to wipe the surprise from my face.

I didn't recognise the lawyer at first. He was tall and harried-looking, his clothes, though neatly pressed, both old and old-fashioned. I could tell he was irritated from the flush in his cheeks and the glares he shot over his shoulder at the guards. When the door was closed he turned to Governor Rogers and dipped into a bow. His eyes flashed towards me. I recognised him then. Recognised him and found myself torn between shocked silence and wild laughter.

Ned Fletcher. The clerk whose name I had stolen when Barnet first took me.

He had been a scrawny, bookish child with bad skin and a nervous stammer. He was still thin but he had filled out somewhat in the last five years.

'Edward Fletcher, sir,' he said. 'I represent Mister William Cormac.' He saw Rogers' blank expression and hurried to elaborate. 'Mistress Bonny's father. We received communication from Captain Barnet that John Rackham's crew had been apprehended, and I was sent here from Charles Town in case Mistress Bonny was also in custody.'

Rogers gave me a hard look.

'Hello, Ned,' I said. 'Good of you to come. How *is* Father?'

Fletcher ignored me. 'We were informed Mistress Bonny is wanted for piracy,' he said. Gone was the nervous stammer. His voice was quiet but resonant, like a preacher's. 'Mister Cormac sent me to discover the nature of these charges.'

'I think it is entirely possible Mistress Bonny has engaged in acts of piracy,' Rogers replied dryly. 'It is not a stretch of the imagination.'

'With all due respect, Governor Rogers, imagination has little place in the law.' Fletcher folded his hands behind his back. 'Are there witnesses?'

'Captain Jonathan Barnet and his crew,' Rogers said.

'And where are these accusers?'

My heart felt as if it would beat right through my skin.

Rogers hesitated. At length, he answered: 'Captain Barnet wrote to me weeks ago, and is expected in Nassau soon. He seems to have been…delayed.'

Relief slipped between my ribs. Perhaps there was a chance after all. For Calico at least. If they had been wrecked, it was even possible Calico and the crew had managed to overthrow Barnet. Maybe they were free even now.

'If there are no witnesses, what charges can possibly be made against Mistress Bonny?'

Maybe there was a chance for *both* of us.

Rogers eyed Fletcher in silence for a moment, his gaze steely. 'She will be held in custody until witnesses can be produced,' he said. 'I am not fool enough to let her escape again.'

'But she will not be tried for piracy until then?'

'That is so.'

It was a small concession, but one I could live with.

'Understand, Mister Fletcher, if no witnesses are eventually produced, Mistress Bonny will be tried for adultery instead. She will be publicly flogged and imprisoned for a length of time, and then she will be returned to her husband.' He looked at me. 'It is not so grave a sentence as I would wish but I will not see your crimes go completely unpunished.' His shoulders were tense, irritation square on his face. Woodes Rogers was a man who was used to getting his own way, and

Fletcher's arrival had ruffled him. I imagined he would have gone ahead and tried me without witnesses if he had been given the time to do so. To tie up loose ends. Rogers was known for negotiating with pirates—it was his arrival that had extended a King's pardon to all those who surrendered—but he had a limit.

That was fine. I didn't need to work with Rogers. I just had to find a way to get out before his threats bore fruit.

Hope was wild, caged in my ribs. I fought to contain it, to keep my features blank. Fletcher's intervention had bought me the only thing I needed: time.

27
BONNY

The rest of the cells being occupied by other men, most of them pirates, Rogers put me in a cellar. Edward Fletcher was permitted to stay with me for a short while. I was chained to an iron loop set into the wall, which made me think they must have had pirates in here before. Fletcher stood on the opposite side of the room. I wanted to thank him for coming, for intervening on my behalf, but he spoke before I could get a word out.

'Your father received your letter.'

'I gathered.'

'I thought you had run out of ways to break his heart, madam,' he said. 'But you have outdone yourself this time.'

What a sanctimonious arse. 'I'm inventive,' I shrugged. 'I thought you were in London.'

'I was.'

'A long way to come for the sake of your former employer's errant daughter.'

'I was in Charles Town when he received the letter. He figured you would be in some sort of legal trouble, so he asked me to come. He had *no* inkling of how deep the problem ran. I have been hearing stories about the female pirate since I arrived here.'

I ignored that. 'And you came when he sent you? Just like that?'

'I owed your father a debt of gratitude.'

I wondered what my father could possibly have done to deserve such loyalty. He had none of mine.

Fletcher cleared his throat. 'I will do my best for you at trial, madam, but from the sound of it, the evidence is damning. You should prepare yourself for the worst.'

'Or you could just let me out.' The cuffs rubbed on my wrists. I shifted, trying to ease the pressure. 'Find a guard, give him a sweet little pouch of coin, get the key. What's one pirate? One *female* pirate.' He opened his mouth but this time I was the one who ploughed on. 'Honestly Fletcher, do you think I was some sort of mastermind in all of this? I was seduced by a pirate and I ran away with him. I didn't actually *do* any pirating. I stayed below for most of it. I was afraid of the crew.'

Fletcher was unmoved by my lies. 'I will see to it that you are properly fed,' he said. 'Make no trouble. Make no attempts to escape. Such a thing can only damage your standing in this case.'

I didn't reply.

'Would you like to write to your father?' he pressed.

'No.'

'Do you have anything to tell me that might be helpful?'

'You could slip me a gun. That would be helpful.'

Fletcher sighed. He went to the door, signalling to the guards to let him out. They did so and the cellar door closed behind him with a heavy thud. I shut him out of my mind as soon as he was gone. He would not be of use.

I sat back against the wall and took stock of my surroundings. It was dark and close in the cellar. There were barrels but they contained nothing but salt and food. No powder or weapons, nothing I could use as a club. There was a heavy lock on the other side of the door. No way to tamper with it.

I sighed and sat against the wall. Fletcher wouldn't help me. And Read…what had happened to him? If the crew had decided to flog him they might have found out about his chest bindings. Maybe he had fought, and been killed. Maybe they threw him over the side as soon as they found him.

He was probably dead. My stomach twisted.

There was a hollow ache in my chest. If I could have found tears I would have shed them.

Thinking of Read led me to thoughts of Calico. Out in the wild waters somewhere. If he was alive perhaps we could find a way to get out. Of course, if he was alive and captive, that meant Jonathan Barnet was still alive and there were the all-important witnesses. Couldn't win either way.

Still, I found myself hoping Calico was alive. Even if it damned me. Even if I swung for it.

Annie. Do you love me?

Ah, Calico. I came to sea with you, didn't I?

The guards considered themselves quite the stage performers, calling insults and lewd suggestions through the door. I thought I recognised one of them. Nassau was a small town and many former rogues seemed to have taken respectable jobs, but it hadn't changed their manners. I bit my tongue. I didn't want them opening the door and coming in, not while I was chained to the damn wall. So long as they stayed on the other side of the door I could ignore them.

But their taunting escalated when they started drinking and one of them began to bark at me. I set my teeth and hunched my shoulders. How long would it be before Barnet arrived in the harbour? How long would it be before a guard took it into his head to break the rules and pass through that door? They could hurt me, rape me, kill me. This was not the way I wanted to die. Chained in a cellar like a dog.

One of them thumped on the door. I twitched back in spite of myself. They laughed. Heart going hard, I stood and tried to steel myself. If they came in they would get a fight from me.

A hiss cut through their laughter: it stopped abruptly. I heard them move away from the door. Clipped footsteps along the stone. A few low comments I couldn't hear. Then the lock clicked and the door swung open again. I squinted against the light.

The blocky form of Woodes Rogers stood in the door. My eyes adjusted to the new light and I watched warily as he stepped into the cellar. The guards were silent now; their governor tolerated no nonsense. He had a gun at his hip and I had the wild, stupid idea to make a grab for it. I crushed the thought before I could act on it. With my feet chained, I'd never get near him.

'Governor Rogers.' My voice was wheezy. I coughed to clear my throat and spat on the flagstones.

Rogers set his jaw. 'Mrs Bonny. Have a little dignity.'

'Have they found Calico?'

He ignored the question. 'I received petitions today on your behalf, Mrs Bonny.'

My heart lightened. The old man must still be trying to get me out of the cell. 'And?'

Rogers sighed. 'My experience has told me that you are clever, deceitful, and utterly without shame.' He held up a hand before I could make a comment. '*However*, I have been convinced that there is someone in Nassau with a claim on you, and I believe him to be capable of keeping your wildness in check this time.'

Someone stood behind Rogers but the light behind made him a silhouette and I couldn't make out any features. Fletcher, I thought. I felt a flare of warmth for the man, chased by a pang of regret: I'd been sharp towards him, ungrateful.

Rogers stepped aside and the other man stepped into the gloom.

'Hello, Annie.'

I thought I could hear the ocean but it was just the blood rushing in my ears.

I couldn't breathe.

His good looks were stained with drinking and weeks of grime. Triumph flushed his cheeks, gleamed in his eyes. He carried a gun. He raked his gaze over me. My courage failed, curled up somewhere deep within me.

'Mister Bonny came to me not long ago to present his own petition.'

Rogers' words swam around me. I struggled to grasp them. I couldn't *breathe*.

'It is a rather unusual situation, to be sure. But the cells in this fort are already stuffed with pirates of greater note than yourself. If Jonathan Barnet returns with evidence against you then you will be taken into custody again. For now the charges are, as Mister Fletcher pointed out, the commoner crimes of adultery and prostitution.'

'Wait…'

'You will be the sole responsibility of your husband from this point, Mrs Bonny, and he has the legal obligation to discipline you as he sees fit.' Rogers' voice was clear and calm. 'I hope you will not give him reason to do so.'

'Don't…'

James walked forward and another man stepped into the cellar, joining him. They took my arms.

'Don't touch me!' I tried to jerk them away but they held tight. One of the guards came in to loose my feet from where they were chained to the wall. I kicked and they pinned my legs, their fingers digging into my thighs, my calves.

'This is the last clemency you will receive from us,' Rogers said over my curses.

They forced my feet into new manacles. The shackles clipping into place pinched my skin bloody. I bucked and threw my head back. The three men pinned me, smirking. Holding me still until Rogers finished speaking.

'If you are brought before us again, madam, you will not find mercy.'

'Don't do this! You *bastard*, don't do this!'

The guard slapped me across the face. My head whipped back. I tasted blood. My neck throbbed.

James caught a handful of my hair and pulled me upright. 'Settle, Annie,' he murmured in my ear. 'I'm taking you home.'

Woodes Rogers stepped aside. 'Take her through the main street,' he said. 'I want to send a message.'

28
BONNY

The sun baked the sandy streets of Nassau. Men and women called their wares from fish markets along the docks. The briny stench of fish was flat on the air, only broken by the occasional sweep of wind off the ocean. Pink conch shells lined the water's edge, scooped out of the water and gutted of the pearly flesh inside. Half-naked children dashed across jetties and pulled small boats out into the harbour waters.

Or I assume they did. I saw none of it.

I was screaming as James and his accomplice dragged me through the main street. The manacles were heavy. My bare feet scraped along the ground, kicking, bleeding, raw. My skin was slick with sweat, my shirt was pulled almost to rags from my struggles. I hollered, called for help, used every curse I knew. I damned them all.

'Adulteress!' James' companion lifted his voice. People gathered on the side of the street in small knots. *Fine entertainment*, I thought as bitter rage curdled my stomach. I dug my heels against the ground and tried to catch my breath. I searched the watching faces for anyone who might help. I looked to the women. Some of them were laughing but others had turned their faces. If they understood, if they felt whispers of compassion, it was not enough to move them. My eyes swung towards the harbour. I could see the familiar mast of the *Jeremiah and Anne* tipping back and forth with the gentle waves. None of her men lined the streets.

They might have done something. They might have helped me.

I was pushed and dragged forward. The manacles were pulled too tight for me to get my balance. My ankles knocked together and I wobbled, then sprawled in the dirt. Knocked my chin on the hard ground. Dust and blood in my mouth.

Something wet hit my face and slid down. Rotten conch flesh. A boy stood at the side of the road with his hand in a wooden bucket. He pulled out another handful of rancid fish and flung it at me. Jeers sprang up through the watching crowd. I dug my fingers into the dust. Spat blood and grime.

James laughed and wrenched me to my feet.

'Not far now,' he said brightly. 'Soon we'll be home, darlin', just you and me. Like old times.'

Like old times.

I tried to blot out the memories but they seeped through me like ink into thin pages. Desperate, frantic, pulled along the street towards James Bonny's shack, I tried to think of Calico. His hands, his crooked smile, those sea-swept eyes. He had stolen me away from James Bonny once before but now he was out on the water, God only knew where; or lost to the ocean forever. James wouldn't let me escape a second time. I was going to die there in that shack.

I looked up and almost fell again. They were taking me east, closer to the waterfront and James' shack at Potter's Cay. It was directly opposite Hog Island, a scrubby, tree-filled stretch of land where pirates and smugglers had done their carousing, and had feasted drunkenly on the wild pigs there. I remembered sitting outside the shack, watching the smoke from their fires curl into the sky. Wondering if Calico was with them; wishing I could join them.

We left the centre of the town. Nassau was on the rise but it was still small, less than three miles from the fort to James' little shack. My muscles ached. I could smell my own fear in the sweat on the air, in the blood that coated the inside of my mouth. The skin around my manacled ankles was bleeding, and I was tired, too tired to fight.

Read was dead.

Calico was somewhere at sea, probably dead too. Bound to swing if they found him.

Annie. Do you love me?

They'd tar him and string him up in a gibbet for the world to see.

Ah, Calico. I came to sea with you, didn't I?

Despair went through me like a fever, like plague. I'd always moved too fast for hopelessness to catch up but now it was seeping into me. I was sick with shame and fear. I had sailed with pirates. I had fought battles and shot men and had a *child.* But James reduced me to the frightened girl I had been four years ago. Sixteen, alone and helpless at the hands of a man who'd pretended to love me.

Shaking, heavy, I hung limp as the two men dragged me the rest of the way to the hut that had flickered through my nightmares for two years.

James' companion shouldered open the door and they hauled me in. It was as dark as I remembered. It reeked of beer, sweat, tobacco, piss. There was one door and one window. No chimney or hearth. Just bare earth and a stained mat on the ground for James to sleep on.

A wooden table and broken chairs. Empty bottles. I stood, swaying, my eyes dancing from the corners where I had cowered and wept. How long would James leave the shackles on my ankles? Could I steal the key from him? I flinched from the thought.

He'd hurt me. If I tried, he'd hurt me.

The door closed behind us. For a bare second all I could hear was the thin wheeze of my own breath. I closed my eyes. Tried to will away the reek of the hut, the sound of James' companion finding a bottle and drinking from it. He handed it to James and went to stand by the door.

James took my chin in his hand. 'Quite the chase you led us, eh, Mrs Bonny?'

I made myself think of the sea.

Of Read.

'You humiliated me, Anne.'

Calico.

'I'm gonna make you hurt for it.'

Annie. Do you love me?

'And when your pirate captain is finally brought to heel, we'll go to the hanging together to watch.'

I hit him.

A jab, hard and fast. His nose crunched beneath my fist and blood spurted out. He snapped back. Roared. Grabbed me and shoved me against the wall of the hut. His hand was at my throat. His friend was shouting, egging him on, and I couldn't breathe. I clawed at him.

I tried to kick but the irons held my feet too close and I couldn't get the swing I needed. I choked. My chest burned.

'Looks like you have some bad habits to break,' James hissed, his mouth framed with blood. He thumped me back against the wall. My teeth clacked together. The world slipped away from me in pieces.

The door slammed open. James turned and his hold slackened on my neck. I gulped air. My lungs couldn't keep up. A gunshot cracked through the air and James' companion staggered to the ground. James released me and went for his gun as I slid down to my hands and knees.

'Reconsider that.'

James froze.

I lifted my head slowly.

Read had a second pistol trained on my husband. His face was calm and intent but there was anger in his eyes. His gaze flicked in my direction.

'Bonny.'

Alive. He was alive. He was alive and armed and he was *there*.

My hands shook as I pushed my hair back out of my face. A sob hollowed out my throat. 'Read.' It hurt to talk. I looked past Read to the men beyond him. For a sick, wild moment I thought it might be the crew of the *Ranger*, my own lads.

'Hello, bonny Bonny.'

I rubbed my throat. 'Darling Darling,' I rasped, meaning it. The stocky musician from the *Jeremiah and Anne* walked over and helped me to my feet.

'Don't you take what's mine!' James snarled.

'Stop us, then,' Read drawled. James twitched, as if he was going to make a lunge for his pistol. Read cocked his own gun. James stilled again and I saw the panic run through him.

Then Read held out the gun to me. Darling's comrades kept their own weapons on James, just in case he tried something.

I waved Darling away and stood on my own. The flintlock was warm from Read's hand, the weight familiar and comforting in my hand. I watched my husband, the man who had wooed and wed me. His begrimed shirt was spattered with blood, his muscles tense. Rage warred with panic in his eyes.

I felt the fear make one last attempt to rise in my chest. Then it withered and died.

'He's not worth the shot,' I said. Everything ached. I was so tired. I turned back to Read. Darling's people lowered their weapons a fraction.

Relief made James stupid. 'Filthy *bitch*,' he rasped as he went for his gun, and I shot him in the face.

The sound of the gun slammed through me as the smoke wisped into the air, as he jerked back and then slumped forward and the blood began to pool around him.

I tried to stay steady but my legs folded under me and I sank to the floor beside the body of my husband. The gun spilled from my hand. The anger and fear that had commanded me for so long were gone. It left me empty, hollow, boneless. James' blood, spreading, touched my hands. Still warm. I shuddered and a deep sob worked its way up from my stomach.

'Give us a moment,' Read said to Darling and his people. 'Stand watch outside, make sure no one comes at the sound of the gun. Spin them a story if you need to.'

They left us alone in the room. Read helped me away from the body. I couldn't stop shaking.

He searched James' body for the key and then sat down to remove my shackles. I kicked them away as soon as they snapped open. Read touched my shoulder. I jerked, then stilled. He wrapped his arms around me and pulled me close.

'You're safe,' he said. His voice was low. 'You're safe, little fellow,' he said again.

I leaned against him and wept like a child.

29
BONNY

I cleaned myself with a bucket of water from outside James' hut. It seemed to take a long time to wash, to make my limbs do anything much. There didn't seem to be an inch of me that didn't hurt.

My shirt was ruined, so when I was done I pulled on James' shirt and coat. They were too big and they reeked, but they would do well enough, and they didn't chafe where my skin was raw. I gathered my hair back in a simple tie and jammed a hat on. I was still wearing skirts but I was beyond caring if anyone knew I was a woman. I scavenged through the hut, taking a belt and a case of shot as well as James' gun. I felt better once I was armed.

Read smiled when he saw me limp out of the shack. 'That's better.'

'Where are...' I cleared my throat. It was still hard to talk. The worst of the bruising was around my neck. Even swallowing was painful. 'Where are the others?'

'They'll be back soon. We'll have to plan from here. You look different from the woman they dragged through the streets but we don't want to take any chances. No taverns or inns.'

'Darling's coves went to get beer, didn't they?'

'Rum, probably.'

I managed a huff of laughter.

Read came inside with me. He shifted the bodies to the side of the room and covered them both with sacks.

'What are we going to do with those?'

'Have to drop them in the harbour when we get a chance,' he said. 'I'll talk to Darling and we'll see what we can arrange.'

He kicked out a chair for me and I eased into it gratefully.

'What happened to you back on the ship, Read?' I asked. 'I thought you were dead.'

'They had the barrels guarded. Couldn't set a proper fire and I couldn't get back to you either. I decided we needed a bit of assistance so I went to the *Jeremiah and Anne* as soon as we docked.'

'How did you know to come here? How did you know I wasn't in the fort?'

'I heard you from the ship. Heard you screaming, saw them dragging you.' That anger flashed back onto his face. 'We came as quick as we could.'

I reached over the table and clasped his hand.

He shrugged. 'I wasn't going to lose you. How bad are you hurt?'

'I don't think anything's broken. Throat feels like hell.'

'Might keep you quiet for once.' He spoke the words lightly but his eyes searched my face. 'What now, Bonny?'

'Now we drink!' Darling shouldered open the door, followed by three other men from the *Jeremiah and Anne*. He stepped over the two corpses and placed a small barrel on the table.

'Nothing like a stiff drink after a good murder,' Read murmured.

'Just so.' Darling pulled up a chair. 'What are we going to do with the bodies?'

'Harbour after dark.'

'A time-honoured tradition,' he agreed.

His lads found some old clay mugs and poured their fill. Darling set out a drink for me. It burned all the way down, a heady mixture of rum, spices, sugar, water and beer. Mostly rum. Darling and his boys were in high spirits. Their captain had extended their shore leave, giving them plenty of time to enjoy freedom in Nassau, and the murder had excited them. They may have started as musicians and performers but these men were pirates. They drank and jested and paid no mind at all to the dead men in the room.

Read and I sat quietly. *What now, Bonny?* It was a good question. We had no way to tell what had befallen Calico and the crew. Nassau was too small for us to move freely. I could tell Read was thinking the same thing. Our eyes met across the table. We both drank.

'I'm not leaving without Calico,' I said at last. 'We've come too far.'

'There's a whole ocean of bad between you and Calico Jack, Bonny.'

'I know. But I have to go after him. I don't want to be without him. I don't expect you to come along with me, mind. You've done enough for me. This isn't your fight.'

'If you're going after Calico Jack, so am I. But we won't be able to do anything until we have more information. It's going to be hard to get that from here.'

'We had an idea about that.' Darling joined the conversation, pouring himself another drink. He wasn't deep into his cups yet, but he already had a ruddy glow about his cheeks. 'We can row you across to Hog Island. You can make camp there, Bonny can recover, and if there's any sight of Barnet coming in with Calico Jack then we'll alert you.'

'Will it be safe there?' Read asked.

'Safe as anywhere. Rogers has Nassau pinned and primped, but smugglers still use the eastern point of Hog Island for their business. No one really lives there but there's still pigs in good numbers and plenty of trees for fuel and shelter.'

Read and I traded a glance. He shrugged; I nodded. 'It'll do until your captain decides it's time to leave,' I said to Darling. 'We'll have to make our decision then in any case.'

There was only so long we could hide in Nassau. Ships went missing out in the wilds all the time, particularly in this season. There was a chance we would simply never know what happened to Calico.

Nassau was quiet at night. Stevedores and whores roamed the docks closer to the middle of the town but we were on the fringes and saw only a few people. A cool breeze cut the thick air. It had been raining all afternoon, since just after we finished drinking. The smell was rich and earthy, a relief from the rotten stench that usually lingered there. The sea, hungry and snarling while the wind was up, had settled into the brooding growl I loved. Lanterns strung along the docks, hanging off ships, gave an eerie glow to the still waters.

Six of us stole through the quiet streets towards the water. We stayed clear of the light and moved along a narrow strip of beach. Read and I wore hats in spite of the darkness, the brims pulled low over our faces for the added shadow. On our shoulders we carried a jolly-boat, overturned. Strapped to the inside were my late husband and his unfortunate friend.

My feet sank deep into the sand, which was still wet from the rain. I struggled to keep my part of the boat level. I was strong enough, but the men were taller than I was and I had to reach up to bear the weight. I didn't mind; the burden of each step reminded me that James Bonny was dead and that put a grim smile on my face.

When we reached the water's edge we flipped the jolly-boat. We ran it into the water up to our knees and climbed in. It felt good to be back on the sea, to feel the world shifting around me again. The familiar sound of the waves licking the side of the jolly. The gentle drag of paddles through the water, pulling us away from the shore. Away from the horror and pain of Nassau.

One of the men sang under his breath, his voice rough but tuneful. I knew the song. It was 'The Ballad of Sir Andrew Barton'. Harwood and Dobbin used to sing it together as they worked, each trying to better the other.

'*Fight on, my men, Sir Andrew says,*
'*A little I'm hurt, but yet not slain…*'

'Keep it quiet, Lillburn,' Darling said. 'Now ain't the time.'

For a while after that the only sound was the sea, and the quiet grunting of men as they rowed. I leaned over the side of the boat, watching the waters. During the day the water was so clear you could tell easily how deep it was just by the changing shade of blue. At night all we had was a line pulled along behind the jolly. I had the rope in my hands, feeling the difference in movement when it ceased to drag along the ocean floor.

I stared into the darkness and it winked back at me.

'Here will do,' I said. 'It's deep.'

We undid the knots securing James and his friend, both wrapped in canvas and weighted with pig-iron Darling had filched from a ballaster's. Read looked across the boat at me. There was a question in his gaze but I didn't know how to answer it. I diverted my eyes to the wrapped bodies.

'Ready, Bonny?' Darling asked.

I shrugged and finished the verse the other man had been singing before. *'Fight on, my men, Sir Andrew says,*

'A little I'm hurt, but yet not slain;

'I'll just lie down and bleed a while,

'And then I'll rise and fight again.'

I stopped there. It still hurt just to talk, let alone sing. Lillburn, the man who had started the ballad, laughed. Darling's beard split with a grin. I grabbed a fistful of canvas and helped the others to haul James' companion over the side. Then we rolled James across the jolly, pulled him up, and sent him down as well. We lowered them gently so as not to make a splash. In moments they were gone, lost to the depths.

No honours. No prayers.

I brushed my fingers over the bruises James had left on my throat. When I glanced around I realised the men were looking at me. I took up an oar. None of us spoke but Darling clapped my shoulder and Read nodded at me. We rowed towards Hog Island and left my husband to the fish at the bottom of Nassau Harbour.

30
BONNY

Darling and his lads left Read and me on Hog Island. We slept beneath a piece of canvas, stretched out between trees and secured with a few short lengths of rope. It wasn't much by way of protection and when the morning rain came in we were drenched. There was no point trying to stay dry, so Read and I sat out just beyond the beach listening to the rain through the trees and watching as the sea gnawed the shoreline. When the sky finally cleared and the tide ebbed we found enough of the pink conches to make a meal. The wood we set out was dry by midday so we cooked the conch flesh and ate. Neither of us said much. After the chaos and fear of the last few days it was a blessing just to sit with him and watch the ships come and go from the harbour.

'We need a plan,' he said at last.

'I know.'

'We need two plans. What are we going to do if your Calico's lost?'

I winced at his bluntness and chewed on some conch flesh. What indeed.

'We take ship on the *Jeremiah and Anne*,' I said. 'If their captain will have us. They sail under Bartholomew Roberts, don't they? Quite a fleet, that. Over fifty ships. And if they don't want us for the long haul I'm sure there'll be a captain who does. We go back to sea.'

'Without him?'

Annie. Do you love me?

I didn't have an answer. It was all well and good to plan for giving Calico up as lost, but Read and I both knew things weren't so simple. When it came to the moment I didn't know if I could leave.

'Look up.' Read's voice sharpened and he stood. I followed his gaze to the waters and saw a small boat headed our way. A man at the oars.

'That's darling Darling,' I said as the boat drew closer. Prickles of unease sprang across my skin. If he'd been coming to drink with us he would have brought the other musicians. But he was on his own.

'Get your axe,' I said to Read, but he was already striding back to our belongings. He caught up his hatchet and a musket, handing the latter to me. We had to be ready to move if there was trouble in Nassau.

I strapped a belt of shot about my torso, slung the musket across my back and secured the flintlock at my belt. It felt good to have two guns on me.

Read and I waded out to meet Darling, steadying the boat as it turned on a wave.

'What's happened?' Read asked.

Darling was out of breath, sweating and flushed from the journey out to the island.

'There's a ship coming in,' he wheezed. 'Looks like the *Albion* to me. She's tore up pretty good but she'll be in the harbour within the next few hours.'

Relief and fear punched into my spine. Maybe our questions would be answered sooner than we expected. I swung myself onto the boat and Read followed. We each took an oar to give Darling a chance to regain his breath.

'A few hours isn't enough time,' I said between my teeth. 'Woodes Rogers will have his men down at the docks as soon as the men disembark. He's not going to let any pirates slip through his fingers. And Barnet...'

'Barnet's going to be careful too,' Read said. 'Especially after losing us in Cuba. He's not going to let anyone take the pirates out of his custody and he is not going to leave for the fort without an escort of guards.'

We rowed, striking evenly, with our hats pulled down—uneasy about being so open on the water in the middle of the day. But there were plenty of boats navigating the little islands around Nassau. Once we were closer to the harbour we were just another vessel and no one paid us much mind.

We pulled into shore and the musicians and players from the *Jeremiah and Anne* met us. We tugged the jolly in and ducked away from the hustle of the harbour. My arms were aching and heavy from the trip in. I shook them out and fidgeted with my flintlock, anxiety starting to set in.

'Where's the ship?' I asked.

'She's coming in from the west,' Darling replied. 'But she's going to have to come around in a loop: the waters are too shallow for her draught and the wind's not doing her any favours. She'll have to tack and come in from the north. And if she wants to anchor near the fort she'll have to come about and head west again.'

'Guardships won't let her put in right in front of the fort,' I said. 'They've had too much trouble with that of late. They won't run any risk of being fired upon.'

'Do we take our chances with an attack?' Read asked.

'Our captain won't allow it,' Darling said. 'He doesn't much mind us larking around with you, Bonny. Even helping you with your husband situation. But he's not going to risk the *Jeremiah and Anne*.'

'That's fair,' I said, though my stomach wrenched with disappointment. It would have been good to have a ship on our side.

'We don't even know your people are alive,' one of the other musicians said.

'How fast is the *Albion* moving?'

'Oh, she's limping along. They've had a bad time of it.'

What did I have? What could I use?

Read stood with his head down, his hands clasped about his axe. His face was tight with thought. Darling scratched his beard. The others all talked in a buzz of whispers. They peppered us with suggestions and questions. Darling waved a hand and started to engage with them. Read raised his eyes and looked at me. I could see in his face that he didn't have a solution.

What did I have?

What could I use?

'Let me think. Just let me think.' I wheeled around, knotting my fingers behind my neck. 'Darling, show me where the ship is. I want to see it.'

He nodded and together we walked up the road, keeping clear of others. The last thing we wanted was to be recognised now. If Calico was still alive on that ship he needed me.

From a small rise in the centre of the town, a hill to the south of the harbour, I could just make out the *Albion* using Darling's scope. No mistaking the big vessel as she lumbered through the waves, leaning badly. She was torn and tattered and it looked like they'd put up a jury-mast to replace one lost or damaged. Whatever she'd been through, I wasn't surprised she was so late coming into Nassau.

I stood on the hill and watched the ships in the harbour, tracking the distance between them and the *Albion*. Clouds were gathering beyond the harbour, the ocean taking sharp edges in preparation for the afternoon rains. Men were working hard and fast down on the docks to finish their tasks, stowing goods before they could be ruined by the storm. The clouds were heavy and I knew the rain would come down in driving sheets.

I took slow, deep breaths. We didn't have much time. But there were other things on our side.

I turned to face Darling.

'Will your men follow me?' I asked.

'Probably not. But they'll follow me and I'm with you.'

I clasped his hand and turned to Read. 'Got an idea.'

'Thought you might.'

'It's mad.' I took a breath. 'Reckless.'

His face broke into a sudden, rare smile. 'Well now. There's a surprise.'

Read and I walked along the docks. I shed the hat and gun-belt for now. It was everything I could do not to run but we didn't want to pull attention to ourselves. We went up and down the small rickety jetties that stretched out to various ships. To anyone else we would look like a sailor and his woman, taking in the sights of the harbour. He even made me stop so we could buy fishing tackle from one of the stalls set up by the water's edge.

'What exactly are we looking for, little fellow?'

'I'll know when I see it.' I went along another jetty. Nassau Harbour could take almost five hundred vessels so long as they were the right type. We were in a hurry but something drew me on in my search.

And then I saw her.

She was small and narrow, built light and fast. Her sails were furled and she was moored, but I knew just from the sight of her that she would run like the Devil when she was out at sea. She wasn't new, exactly. I could see weathering on her beams and some old damage to her bowsprit, which had a lean on it, a little to the larboard side. We could fix that. And she was clean. Her hull was smooth and she would slice through the waves. I could see some guns at her deck; probably no more than six. No good for an outright battle; enough to give us options.

In spite of our hurry, in spite of the urgency I felt, I was pinned to the spot just from the sight of her. The *William.* My father's name. A smile curled around my lips. It felt like God's jest. And a finger pointing the way forward.

'This one?'

I couldn't tear my eyes away from her, not even to look at Read. I nodded.

We stepped out of the way as a sailor passed us by, leaving the ship with a barrel on his shoulder. Read hailed him. I adjusted the kerchief at my neck, disguising the bruises James had left there, and I kept my head low.

'Who does this ship belong to?' Read asked the man, his voice light and friendly.

'Captain John Ham,' the sailor replied. 'You seeking passage?'

'We are.' Read slipped an arm about my waist. 'Looking to get to Cuba.' He lowered his voice. 'My girl here, her parents aren't too fond of me. We plan to marry in Havana. God willing, by the time we get back here they'll have calmed some and her father won't be so much in the mind to take his fists to me.'

The sailor laughed. 'Well, we're taking passengers,' he said.

'Any chance a couple can take a look at her before we take to the journey?'

The sailor handed the barrel to another man. 'Let me show you around.'

I flashed Read a triumphant look. His eyes were warm. We followed the sailor aboard.

31

BARNET

The town of Nassau came into view, a stain on the green and white shores of New Providence Island. Barnet stood at the bow of the *Albion*, one hand clasped about a stay. The ship creaked and groaned with every large wave, her timbers and beams shivering with the strain of the distance they had come.

Just a few more miles. She could last a few more miles.

Barnet took a long breath. It was almost over. Soon the pirates would be taken, his burden lifted, and he would be able to rest before starting anew. Before finding another name to pursue.

Not before he saw these men hanged, though. He would wait long enough for that.

Gulls wheeled and keened overhead. Grey crept through the sky. Barnet tried to curb his impatience. They would reach the harbour just before the storm did. The danger was past. He would not make the same mistake twice. He would not let Calico Jack and his men out of his sight until they were in the custody of Governor Rogers.

The *Albion* was too large and unwieldy to take straight into port from the west. Nassau Harbour was deep between Nassau and Hog Island but from the west and east it was shallow in patches, and Barnet did not trust the ship's steering when she had sustained so much damage. They tacked instead, carefully taking the ship around a small island so they could come in from the north. Barnet thought bitterly of the impression they *should* have made: gliding in to the harbour resplendent, a gleaming sword of God. Restoring order. Instead, they hobbled across the waves like common harbour-drift.

Yet another rebuke he could add to the pirates' account.

He turned away from the bow and walked down the companionway to the brig. It was a pitiful crowd of pirates who remained there. Just eleven of them from the original crew of thirty.

They were thin and haggard. At first they had been boisterous, defiant, calling out insults and threats to the crew even as they were fed and given water. But the weeks of hardship had subdued them and now they just watched him with wary, hate-filled eyes. It stuck in Barnet's craw that they had lost so many. He had wanted to see them all swing.

'We approach Nassau,' he said. 'When we arrive you will be transported to the fort where you will be imprisoned and questioned. Governor Woodes Rogers will see you put to trial, and justice will finally be done. In your situation, I would bend my mind to prayer. Cast yourselves upon God's mercy; Woodes Rogers will spare you none.'

The tall slave, Isaac, spat. The boy named Harwood folded his hands behind his head and rocked. His friend, Dobbin, sat slumped against the bars. He had scarcely spoken since the carnage on the beach near Havana. Barnet knew all of these men by now. He knew their names, their ages, their stations on the ship. He had had many of them beaten and interrogated across the weeks at sea. It was the one thing he'd had some control over while the *Albion* was at the hands of the elements.

Before he turned away from the brig he looked over at Rackham. The pirate met his gaze. He was bruised, one eye swollen shut and his lip crusted with blood. The stubble on his face had become a straggly beard. And there was no defiance left in him. The striding captain in motley was no more. He had been beaten and bowed, and finally brought to heel. After a moment Rackham lowered his eyes.

Barnet smiled.

The roar of cannons. A black flag rising through the smoke and flames. A skull, sporting an earring and bandana, set above crossed bones. Men swung belaying pins and fought valiantly, and Jonathan wanted to be among them, should have been among them, but he was frozen. There were so many. He ran through the decks of the ship, stooped low. Like a coward. He found his way through the bowels of the vessel, down into the bilge where the sour water and the rats waited. It was almost too small for him. He had to crouch, thighs burning and heart beating on his ribs. There was a lull. He could hear the quiet slip and hiss of the foul water in the bilge, the squeak of rats, the dull rasp of the waves against the other side of the hull.

Then the screaming started.

His smile fixed, then slowly faded. These memories, these dark thoughts, had been driven from his mind years ago. Why did they plague him now, so close to victory?

A test of faith, perhaps.

Barnet was not lacking in faith.

The wind was up when he returned to the upper decks. The crew, exhausted from their long passage, worked the lines in silence. Barnet did not know how to express his admiration for their stoic courage through these difficult weeks at sea. He would have to show his appreciation from his coffers, light as they were these days.

They came into the harbour from the north. Barnet's eyes sharpened. Smoke rising from Nassau. He leaned on the rail.

'Keep to the east,' he told the helmsman. 'Looks like there's a fire on the docks.'

'Should we anchor further out?' Hutch, the bosun, asked.

'No. I will not risk rowing the pirates in to shore. It is no great matter. The rain will fall soon and make short work of any blaze.'

The fire did not look devastating, but the harbour was full enough that it was passing from ship to ship. Men scurried across jetties and docks with pails of water, trying to protect their own vessels. Barnet's crew gave the commotion a wide berth, bringing the *Albion* in to a quiet mooring on the eastern side of the harbour. It meant a greater distance to the fort, but Barnet did not intend to take the pirates in until he had an armed escort in any case. For now they could stay in the brig.

The men lowered the anchor and fitted the gangplank. The crew gathered on the upper decks. There was longing in their eyes. The hard weeks at sea had taken a toll on them. Barnet knew all they wanted was to go ashore, find wine and women, and forget the rough journey they had endured. He would be happy to help them finance this endeavour, but not yet. They could wait a little longer for fort guards to relieve them of their captives.

The women were screaming.

Constance—

Barnet blinked the rain out of his eyes as it started to fall. He watched as a small knot of men approached the *Albion*. They were clad in uniform—like many of Rogers' guards, a shabby and piecemeal uniform—and they looked as though they had been battling the fire. They were flushed and sweating and one of the men seemed to have singed off half his beard.

'Captain Barnet?' the man called from the bottom of the gangplank. 'Permission to come aboard, sir?'

'Identify yourself.'

'Corporal Drake, sir. We have come from Governor Rogers to escort your cargo to the fort.' The man's bearded face grew apprehensive. 'You…you *do* have a cargo of pirates, sir?'

'Of course I do,' Barnet snapped, nettled. He did not need the reminder that he had lost so many of them in the fray on the beach and the voyage that followed. 'Come aboard.'

There were eight men in all. Rough-cut soldiers, but well armed and strong enough looking to handle themselves with the pirates. Barnet led them down to the brig. His own men had already bound the pirates in a line, hands to neck. The elderly slave, a man they called Old Dad, struggled to stand, swaying from side to side. He was bleeding from the temple; Barnet assumed he had given the crew some trouble.

'This is it?' Drake asked. 'We were led to believe…'

'This is the entire crew,' Barnet replied through clenched teeth.

'We were expecting at least thirty men.'

'This is the entire crew.'

Drake swallowed and did not pursue it further. Wisely.

Barnet unlocked the brig and the guards herded the pirates out. It was slow going up the companionway—roped together, hands bound, the pirates slipped and struggled on the wooden ladder. Barnet felt a twist of vindictive pleasure to hear them choke and splutter as they climbed onto the upper decks.

'Captain?'

Hutch stood with a group of crewmen.

'Not now, Hutchinson.'

'Captain, are we dismissed?'

Barnet narrowed his eyes. Usually he would have punished such impertinence.

'The quartermaster will distribute the pay,' he said at last. 'Do not disgrace the good name of the *Albion*, and be back here by tomorrow morning for muster. I will instruct you then as to the length of your shore leave.' He was gratified to see relieved smiles leap onto the crew's faces. A good leader knew when to loosen the reins.

'We'll take them from here,' Drake said. 'The governor will see you tomorrow to commend you, and to discuss your reward.' A smile crossed his face. 'Congratulations, Captain Barnet. It has been a long journey, but these men will meet the full force of the law. You have served your King honourably.'

'With all due respect, corporal, I would like to personally see these men brought before Governor Rogers. It will give me great satisfaction to see this through to the end.'

Drake's smile faded. 'I can assure you captain, we will deliver this charge safely to the governor.'

'I do not doubt your competence corporal, but I am loath to leave my post until I have been formally relieved of it. I have lost good men to these people. Perhaps you will think it petty, but I wish to see them brought to justice personally.'

Drake hesitated, then gave a stiff nod. 'Very well.' He turned and jerked the rope attached to Rackham's neck. 'Move!'

The pirate stumbled forward a step. He did not raise his eyes. He drew a slow, shaking breath, then trudged after Drake with the walk of a man bound for the gallows. The other pirates followed. They kept their heads low, even the men who had been most defiant at the beginning. Barnet walked alongside them, his hand on the hilt of his sword.

The docks were filled with smoke. Though the rain had started it was not yet enough to douse the flames. Men ran across their paths with buckets, halting them time and time again. The smoke choked them all, pirate and hunter alike. Barnet found himself reaching for a kerchief in his pocket to hold over his mouth. The procession made it only a short way towards the fort before Drake stopped, frustrated.

'It's no good,' he said. 'We'll have to go around.'

Barnet coughed and cleared his throat. His eyes stung from the smoke. 'The most direct route possible,' he urged.

'Of course, captain.' Drake's eyes were red-rimmed, streaming. He took them inland a short way, away from the harbour and into Nassau. There was a strong wind coming in off the sea but the short wooden buildings gave them some protection from the smoke that lashed across the town. They moved into the shadow of a deserted street. Barnet guessed most of the town was down at the docks trying to salvage their businesses.

One of the younger pirates stopped. Dobbin. He was towards the front of the line and the other men stalled behind him as he coughed helplessly, bent double. Barnet reached across and grabbed the length of the rope just in front of the man's neck, yanking it hard.

'Move,' he snapped.

Dobbin staggered.

'Let him alone!' The small, wiry slave, Old Dad, tried to push forward from the back.

Barnet turned and cracked his fist across the old man's face. The slave fell back. Dobbin's wheeze cut into the silence.

The pirates stopped walking. Rackham stood at the front, his head low and his shoulders tense. A ripple ran through the men.

'Keep moving,' Corporal Drake said from the front of the line.

The old slave spat out a tooth. 'Bastard,' he hissed at Barnet.

'You heard the man!' Barnet snarled. 'Walk!'

Rackham squared his shoulders. No more words passed among the pirates but they followed their captain's lead, straightening. Barnet put his hand on his gun. He wanted to deliver the pirates to Woodes Rogers, to justice, to the noose. But if he had to shoot them down in the street, he would.

'Move now or I will shoot!'

The women were screaming.

Constance—

'Put your weapon down, Captain Barnet.'

Barnet's gun wavered.

Drake had a musket trained on him.

So did the other guards.

'What is this?' He spoke between his teeth. Sweat prickled on his palms, on his brow.

'A rescue. Lower your gun, captain.'

It was over. The ship had been gutted of its wares. Beaten and bleeding, Barnet had been found cowering in the bilge and now he knelt on the upper deck with the other survivors. The pirates surrounded them, jostling one another and laughing.

Constance was just a few feet away, sprawled across the deck on her stomach. Her nails were red with blood from where she had clawed at her attackers, her clothes torn from their outrages. More than anything Barnet wanted to drape his coat over her, to afford her some dignity in death.

But he could not move.

He was so afraid.

Corporal Drake walked forward and slashed the ropes binding the pirates. His men, the men who had disguised themselves as Rogers' guards, gathered about them in a tight knot. They put their arms about the pirates, steadied the men who were faltering on their feet. The pirates were confused, stunned into silence, but they accepted the help that was offered.

John Rackham, newly freed, flexed his hands and rubbed his wrists, his eyes gleaming as he turned to face Barnet. There was a bright triumph in his face, a light Barnet had thought to be extinguished.

Enemies on all sides.

'I will say it one more time, captain.' The imposter took a step closer. 'Put the gun *down*.'

Panic and rage warred in Barnet. His crew was too far off to be summoned, the men from the town were all out at the docks. There was no one to come to his aid. By the time the soldiers arrived from the fort, it would be too late.

There was no chance of shooting his way out. But he would not surrender to pirates. Not again.

Never again.

He swung his gun around and pointed it at Rackham.

If he was to die, he would die doing the Lord's work.

32
BONNY

As Read and I left the *William* the smoke was already rising from the docks. Darling and his lads had set the fires strategically, working fast to strike and run. The *William* was far enough to the west that she was in no danger, and she would be well clear of the guards from the fort when they came to help combat the blaze.

We stood on a jetty in the shadow of another vessel and watched as the *Albion* groaned into the harbour. She looked to be in a bad way. Her hull was honeycombed with bore-holes from hundreds of tiny teredo worms. Her sails were in tatters and one of the masts had been snapped halfway up. They had replaced it with a jury-rig, just enough to help them limp to a safe port, but it leaned badly to port.

Desperate to see my lads, I watched men move across the deck, searching for Calico. Isaac. Old Dad. Dobbin and Harwood. I sucked in a breath of air and forced it out again slowly. The gun in my hand was slippery from sweat. The only thing stopping me from running out of hiding and right onto that ship was Read's solid presence, an anchor at my side.

Read knocked my shoulder lightly and nodded towards the docks. Darling and his men approached the *Albion*, dressed in the closest approximation of guard uniform they could dredge up at such short notice. Putting their acting skills to good use. I wanted to be there with them. I wanted so badly to be at their side but there was no way I could get any closer without being recognised.

Please, God, let him be alive. Let them all be alive.

Darling shouted something up to the ship. I could just make out Barnet standing at the prow. There would be no saving him if he had killed my Calico. My hand tightened about the gun.

Darling and his men went aboard. They spoke with Barnet briefly, then disappeared. There was nothing we could do but wait. Hope and fear gathered in a knot about my throat, pulling tighter and tighter until my breath was nothing more than a thin, high whistle. There were shouts from further along the docks. The blistering smell of smoke carried on the wind. A wave slapped against the jetty and it swayed beneath our feet.

And then, there they were. Bound, bowed, trudging up onto the deck. I grabbed Read's arm. With their heads down, I couldn't quite tell which of our lads they were—except Isaac, at the back, the tallest of all of them. I squinted, desperately trying to work out if Calico was among them.

'Steady, Bonny,' Read murmured. I was holding him too tight. I pried my hand away and searched the deck, waiting for more of the men to come out. There were only eleven so far. Less than half our crew.

'Where are the others?' I hissed.

Read didn't have an answer. Darling and Barnet spoke, then started to walk down the gangplank, taking the eleven crewmen with them.

Eleven?

Grief knocked me square in the chest.

Just eleven.

But there was no time for tears. No time to wonder what happened to the boys, whether they'd died quick or slow, no time to figure out who we'd lost and who we could still save. Darling and his men were taking our lads along the docks. They passed our jetty and I drew back into the shadows, scanning the faces.

Relief weakened me. Calico. My Calico was at the front of the line. He was thin and unshaved, his head low and his shoulders slumped. He looked like the ocean had spat him up. But he was alive.

I could bear any other loss so long as he was still alive.

Barnet was with them. *Spiteful,* I thought. He wanted to see every moment of suffering. Rage twisted in me and ground through my bones. He would get his reckoning.

He'd left his men on the ship. Some of them came down in small knots but they went west, doubtless seeking out taverns where they could rest and eat and keep company with whores. Read and I waited until they were clear, then ducked out from the underside of the ship and started to follow Darling and the procession of men. They were far ahead of us but we kept them in sight. The smoke grew thick and smothering, worse for a while as the rain started to beat down the fire. The wind wasn't enough to cut it. I lifted the kerchief I had around my neck, using it to protect my face. Read kept pace with me, steady and relaxed. He'd worn the axe strapped to his back until now. There was something deadly about the casual way he swung it: lightly, to the beat of his steps.

One of the crewmen stopped. I couldn't tell who it was but a weak, hacking cough carried back to us. Barnet strode to the line and yanked the rope. Old Dad's voice rose. There was a hard snap and I saw Old Dad stumble back, almost to the ground, dragging on the man before and behind him. Our lads stopped walking. Barnet put up his gun.

I jerked and almost ran out, but Read clapped a hand on my shoulder. He held me steady as we waited, standing in the lee of a small building. My heart was beating so hard I thought it would bruise me.

Darling's men revealed themselves; Barnet didn't lower his gun. They kept talking but he didn't waver and I knew suddenly that he wouldn't surrender. That he would take as many pirates to the grave as he could, no matter what befell him.

'Bonny—'

Barnet's gun swung to point at Calico. I wrenched away from Read and ran forward, firing as I ran.

The shot cracked through the air.

The gun flew out of Barnet's hand.

He dropped to his knees, clutching at his wrist as blood spattered the ground. Read was at my side a breath later, skidding into Barnet and tackling him to the dirt. I grabbed the gun he had dropped and wheeled around. His was primed and I pointed it at him. I didn't dare take my eyes off him, not even to look over at Calico.

Read wrestled Barnet's arms behind him and pinned him with a knee in the small of his back. Barnet struggled, wild, but he stopped when he looked up and recognised me.

'Surprise.' I bared my teeth. 'You have him, Read?'

Barnet twisted, only just realising who it was who had him on the ground. His face contorted with rage. He bucked again but Read had him solidly down. Moments later, Isaac was there as well, adding his weight. I opened my mouth to say something but Calico grabbed my shoulders and spun me around, and his arms were about me, and I couldn't breathe.

I didn't care who saw.

A sob caught in my chest and threatened to pull loose. I held on, feeling how thin and frail he was since the last time I'd seen him. This was not the bold pirate who had rushed into battle so many times, nor the man who had stolen me away from Nassau. But he was still my Calico.

I could have stayed like that for the rest of my life. I clutched Calico tighter for one moment then stepped away from him.

'We have to get out of Nassau.'

He was tired, frayed by grief, but a smile touched the corners of his mouth. 'I take it you have a plan.'

'I have a ship.' I took in the faces of the other lads for a moment. They were in a bad way but they gathered close. Harwood reached over and clapped my shoulder. I glanced over at Read and Isaac, then took the manacles from where they'd been secured to my belt. We cuffed his feet.

'Harlot,' he snarled at me. There was a cut above his brow and it bled into his eye. 'I'll see you *hang!*'

'Doubt it,' I murmured. I considered killing him; it would be easy. And he'd cut down more than half of our crew. He deserved it.

I held the gun against his head. Read took in a sharp breath. I knew how he felt about cowardice.

Barnet steeled himself. He squared his shoulders and lifted his chin. Prepared to go nobly to his death at the hands of a pirate.

I leaned in and spoke in his ear. 'Remember that *I* chose to let you live, Barnet.'

He opened his mouth to speak but I cracked my gun against the back of his head.

A murmur went through our small crew. They wanted him dead. But the sound fell away as I turned to face them.

'We'll take him with us, maroon him somewhere. The pirate way.'

Calico smiled grimly. 'What's the plan, Bonny?' he asked.

'It's getting dark. We need to get down to the docks and onto our ship.'

'Where did you get a ship?' Harwood asked.

'It's not ours yet.'

'There it is,' Isaac muttered.

'We'll follow your lead,' Calico said. The words took me by surprise, fanned warmth up into my cheeks.

Hurriedly, I turned to Darling. The bearded man stood smiling, his men at his back. I held out a hand to him. Clasped the hand that had pushed my husband's body into the deep.

'Darling Darling.' My voice was warm.

He squeezed my hand. 'Bonny Bonny.'

'My thanks. We owe you.'

'We'll remember it if we ever need you. Now, get out of the harbour safely. And make sure you cause plenty of trouble.' He paused, then turned to one of his lads and took a sheet of black cloth from him. He pressed it into my hands. 'It's not exactly what you're used to but it'll do until you're established. Fly it true. I'll see you on the waves. We're going to set fire to Barnet's ship.'

He gestured to his men and they went off the other way. I was sorry to see him go but we had no time to linger over farewells. The rains were sweeping in now. The fire on the docks would be all but quenched and soon the governor's men would be all over Nassau in search of our lads.

Dobbin was unsteady on his feet so I put an arm about his shoulders and helped Harwood as we started towards the docks. Isaac and Read carried Barnet between them. And I didn't let Calico out of my sight, not for one moment.

33
BONNY

The *William* had sailed out a short way to keep clear of fire damage but she still lay close to shore. We took to the underside of a jetty, waiting there until the cover of dark was upon us and the rain was coming down in sheets. Then we pushed a stolen jolly-boat out onto the water and struck out for the *William*. It didn't take long, but even that short length was too much for some of the lads. Dobbin and Old Dad were in a bad way. I could hear the breath whistling in their lungs and there was something I didn't like about the set of their eyes. Paddy Carter had a dirty bandage about his leg; he limped all the way to the beach, helped along by George Fetherstone. Isaac was stoic but I could see he was struggling to keep our pace. In the end the rowing was down to Read and me, and the solid Richard Corner.

Calico sat nearby and even when I wasn't looking I felt his eyes on me.

The waters were rocky but quiet. Everyone was picking for salvage at the shore, trying to recoup their losses. We made short work of the distance to the *William* and climbed aboard, lugging Barnet's limp form after us. The boys weren't gentle with him; they dumped him on the decks and Isaac stood over him with a gun in case he roused.

The two men on watch weren't even on the deck. I had seen a crate of wine in the captain's cabin when the mate showed me through earlier and I didn't doubt they were sampling it while the owner was ashore. I took my pistol and Barnet's sword, which was a fancy thing, but sharp enough. Richard Corner led the lads around the ship, getting us underway. Calico gave orders in a low, terse voice. Once the boys were scattered and working he looked at me.

'There are guardsmen?'

'Just two. Read and I can manage them.'

His face hardened and he jerked his head in a nod. I exchanged a glance with Read and we went down together towards the cabin. Read knocked my shoulder. I slammed open the door to the cabin.

'On your feet!' I shouted. The men lurched up, startled. Read was over my shoulder, ready with a gun in case there were any surprises. I showed my teeth. 'Let's make this nice and easy. If either of you tries to resist, I'll blow out your brains.'

They didn't have weapons and they were wine-softened. One started to protest but the other dug him hard in the ribs and they fell to silence.

'Delightful.' I jerked the pistol. 'Out you come. Read, the wine can go to our lads when we're done, wouldn't you say?'

'Seems fair.'

'You.' I waved the gun between the two men. 'We're reasonable. You do as you're told, don't stir an inch, and we'll set you off safe when we're in the clear. Not a sound, understand?'

They were honest merchant sailors and they didn't give us any sort of a fight. We locked them in the brig, which wasn't much more than a few feet in either direction, and then we went back above to join Calico and the others. Richard Corner stayed behind on guard. We didn't need a large crew to get the *William* underway, and that was a lucky thing. Half the lads were sitting on the deck with their elbows resting on their knees and their heads cradled in their hands.

'Haul in the anchor and let loose the other cable,' Calico said to Isaac and Richard Corner. He didn't need to say anything to me. I was already in the rigging, Read at my side, to let the sail out a fraction. Not much—just barely enough for steerage. We went south-west, sliding through the harbour and past the fort. If I'd had my way we would have had no lanterns but in the rain and darkness we needed them, especially in the shallow harbour waters. There were guardships close. It would look to them as though we were simply drifting, perhaps in some fix, but I didn't want to take any chances. If we sped out of the harbour we would rouse suspicion. If we went too close to the fort we'd be stopped and possibly searched. And if they knew about our escape there was no way they'd let us sail away from Nassau.

'Annie.'

Calico didn't need to say any more than my name. Read and I stayed as we were in the rigging, hands on the ropes. Isaac was at the helm, his feet planted and his hands on the wheel. He guided the ship subtly, letting the waves carry us in a gentle weave. Richard Corner was below on the guns. We wouldn't last in a firefight but we weren't going to be taken again. Better to go down than be strung up.

The air still smelled of smoke, though the rain had dampened the scent and the fires were all out now. Calico stood at the prow, straight-backed despite the driving sheets. Somewhere along the way he had lost his coat. He looked strange going into danger without it.

'Bonny,' Read murmured in my ear. 'Pay attention.'

I jumped, then shot him a foul look, blinking rain out of my eyes and adjusting my grip on the rope.

'You're too close!' The voice came to us over the waves from one of the guardships. My heart stammered, then beat hard on my ribs. It was cold in the rigging, under the onslaught of the rain, but I was sweating.

'We know!' It was Calico who called back, leaning on the rail. 'Anchor cable parted. We've drifted all the way through the harbour. We're working on it!'

If they didn't believe us, we were all dead. If we made a single wrong move we would be fired upon by all three nearby guardships and we'd be nothing more than a pile of charred boards and broken bodies at the bottom of the harbour. A feast for the same fish that had fattened themselves on my husband's corpse. My chest was tight. I looked to Read for reassurance. He watched with unshaken focus, his hands wrapped tight on the ropes.

A rough laugh sounded across the waves. 'Not a good night for you, is it?'

I caught my breath, shaken with relief. Read's shoulders eased. I could hear the warmth in Calico's voice when he called back to them.

'Can you help us?'

More laughter. 'Not likely. You got yourselves into it, and we've had enough problems tonight. Mind, you're headed out to sea, lad. Make sure you right yourselves, or you'll bump into Florida before you know it.'

They laughed again as we drifted past them. The sound of their mirth carried as we floated towards the mouth of the harbour. I waited until Calico looked up at us. Then Read and I worked fast, letting out the sails. They snapped out and filled instantly, taking with the strong winds.

And the *William* sped past the lip of the harbour like the word of God.

She was faster than I could have imagined, her smooth hull shearing through the water and scudding ahead of the waves. As the rushing air filled my lungs I was taken with the mad, giddy desire to laugh. I scrambled down the rigging to Calico. I wanted to touch him, to kiss him, but I held back.

'You've forgotten something,' he said to me, his eyes still on the harbour as it receded behind us. His voice was low and rough.

'What?'

He turned then, one eyebrow arching. 'I would have thought you'd want to run our colours.'

I remembered, then, the black square Darling had given us.

'We'll be screaming our name to anyone who sees us,' I said slowly, testing the waters.

'It's a good name,' he countered. 'And now we have a good ship to match.'

I gathered a handful of his shirtfront and pressed my lips against his. Then I ran for the belongings we'd gathered below and found the black cloth. I brought it back above, climbed up the swaying rigging and met Read there at the mainmast.

'Is that wise?' he asked, not needing to ask what it was I held in my hands.

'Perhaps not.' I finished securing the flag and watched as it whipped out in the wind. Darling Darling and his men must have fashioned it while we were waiting to hear news of Calico. It was roughly sewn but the emblem was clear, white blazing against the black: a skull over two crossed swords. Our flag. Our sign.

If anyone from Nassau Harbour saw us, if anyone realised we had slipped out through Woodes Rogers' fingers, it was too late. We set the two hapless guards from the *William* off on a jolly-boat and let them row into shore. It would take them many hours and that would be more than enough time for us to be in the clear.

We did not send Barnet with them. I must have hit him harder than I thought, because he didn't stir until the guards were off the ship. By then he was secure in the brig. I peered through the bars at him as he stirred and groaned: he was a different creature, rumpled and bruised, stuffed in there with only the rats, and a bucket to piss in.

I couldn't wipe the smile off my face.

Barnet craned his neck as Read came down the companionway. He blinked like a sleepy child, mouth slack. Then he dragged himself upright. His eyes grew wild.

'Pirates!' he hissed.

Read came to stand beside me. I had a hundred jibes to throw at Barnet but Read's presence quieted me and instead we just stood there, looking at our conquered enemy. I wondered if Read felt pity for the man; his face was as smooth and inscrutable as ever. I leaned my shoulder against his.

'Annie.'

Calico stood at the companionway. There was tension in his voice. I smiled at him but no grin answered mine.

'Is he conscious?'

'Conscious but witless,' I said.

'We're dropping anchor.' He joined us at the bars of the brig, hatred tightening his shoulders. He stared in at Barnet with an anger I'd never seen in him. I wanted to reach for his hand, to give him some comfort, but he moved away from me as soon as Isaac and George Fetherstone came down the steps.

I swallowed my discomfiture. Now was not the time.

Read took out his gun and held it steady on Barnet as Isaac and Fetherstone unlocked the brig. They hauled Barnet to his feet, bound his hands and feet, and dragged him to the open decks. Our crew waited there and a pang went through me. Seeing them gathered together drove home how few we were now.

No one said a word as we hustled Barnet into the remaining jolly-boat, already winched over the side of the *William*. Calico, Read, Corner and I clambered in, and Isaac and the other lads lowered the jolly. We rowed out to a small spit of land. There wasn't much room there even for trees. Nothing to eat. No fresh water.

Barnet muttered the whole way. It took me a while to realise he was praying. Read and I exchanged a glance. Prayer was the only hope Barnet had out here. It would be an act of God if any ships passed by before he died of thirst or hunger.

Or took the other option we were giving.

Read stood by the jolly, holding it still from the tug of the wave while we hauled Barnet up the beach. He struggled and kicked, his voice rising in a ragged shout. Richard Corner and Calico flung him into the sand. He tried to rise but Corner struck him over the head with a belaying pin. Barnet slumped back to the ground, senseless once more. We removed the bonds from his hands and feet. There was no point to them now. Then Calico placed a pistol in the sand. According to tradition, it would be loaded with shot. Just the one. Just enough to give Barnet the choice. It was nothing like mercy, but it was the pirates' way.

Calico straightened and I saw a glimmer of satisfaction in his eyes. He met my gaze and I wondered, briefly, whether he had loaded the gun.

I didn't question him. Calico was our captain, and some things were his decision after all. I just followed as we took to the jolly, pulled out to sea, and returned to the *William*.

We left Barnet to choose his death.

34
BONNY

'You're a woman, then?'

The wind had dropped and we sat about the decks, eating a meal Paddy Carter and George Fetherstone had managed to scrape together from the supplies in the hold. Conversation had been sparse, no one commenting directly on my skirts or the embrace Calico and I had shared, but now Dobbin spoke up. He was pale, his eyes ringed with bruised flesh. It would be some time before he was his old self again but the escape and food had given him some renewed energy.

Read sat with his shoulder leaning against mine, and I felt tension gather in his arm. I nudged him, then flashed Dobbin a smile and ducked into a mock curtsey.

'God's blood.' He sat back a moment, then looked at me, dismayed. 'You've seen me *piss!*'

'Calm down, Dobbin. There wasn't a lot to see.'

Harwood chortled around a mouthful of food. Old Dad shot me a sly smile that made me think he'd had his suspicions long before this. I winked at him and he gave a short bark of laughter that turned into a hacking cough.

Some of the other lads swapped glances and didn't comment. Unease crept through me. I had some work to do, to get their allegiance. I hadn't forgotten that one or two of these boys had been Sedlow's cronies. Men who had threatened to drown me.

I glanced around the deck for Calico but he was still in the captain's cabin, charting our course. Picking at my food, no longer hungry, I was lost in thought until Read finally spoke his mind.

'Bonny.'

'Mm?'

'You know these men.'

'As well as I know anyone.'

'Are we safe with them?'

Were we? I considered it. I imagined they would have questions, once they had time to recover from their hardships. Once we were out at sea for long hours, in the sun and in the storms. Still, they had been happy enough to let me fight alongside them and they could put it aside for now. That boded well for me, and for Read as well.

I nodded towards Isaac, out on the helm. Solitary and quiet as ever. Keeping us on-course.

'See the big fellow over there?' Isaac was one of the few crewmen taller than Read himself. 'That's Isaac. He doesn't like me much.'

'I wonder why.'

I ignored that. 'Personal feelings aside, Isaac is solid as any anchor, and he's well-liked by the crew. You should talk to him. Bring him something to eat.'

Read glanced over at Isaac, then back at me. He nodded. 'I might. Go on, now. Go see your Calico.' He went over to Paddy to get some food for Isaac and I left them, making my way to Calico's cabin.

I felt strangely nervous. For the first time in years, I actually knocked.

'Come in, Isaac.'

I cracked the door. 'Not Isaac.'

He was going through the charts left on the *William*, seeing if there was anything that could be of use to us. Anything else, we would sell. His hands were braced on the small table in the cabin and again I thought to myself how tired he looked. This was not my wild sea-captain, the man who had stolen me away from Nassau.

I slipped inside and closed the door behind me.

'You're not beholden to me.' He spoke before I could say a word. 'You owe me nothing. I helped you away from Nassau, you helped me away from Barnet. We're even.'

'A fair few things happened between those two events,' I pointed out. He didn't say anything so I went on, trying to soften my voice. 'I'm not here because I feel like I owe you, Calico. This isn't a transaction.'

'You did a good thing, coming back for us. Saved all of our lives, what's left of us. Found us this ship. We'll see you safely to Hispaniola.' He paused. 'You and that fellow. Read.'

Folding my arms, I leaned on the door. 'Just to Hispaniola?'

'I assume the two of you will step off there.'

'That's not the plan.'

He finally looked up from the charts. Hot anger and hurt flashed through his eyes. 'You need to change plans, then,' he said. 'Because if the two of you stay on my ship I'm going to have to take him in a duel. And I'll kill him, Annie. I will.'

I sighed. 'Calico. For God's sake. I love you, but sometimes you're as dumb as a sardine.'

He stilled. 'What?'

'You think Read and I are lovers, is that right?'

'Wait—'

'Read's dear as a brother to me. I have no secrets from him, he's saved my life on more than one occasion. It forges a particular sort of friendship.'

'Wait, Annie—'

'But we're not lovers. And if you challenge him to a duel I won't ever forgive you. Besides, I stole this ship. Rightfully I own it. You're just the captain. You're not throwing me off.'

'You love me?'

Hard to tell if he'd even heard the rest of it. His hands gripped the table so tight his knuckles paled. There was hope and fear on his thin face. This brave, reckless, stupid man who had stolen ships, and me, and my heart.

I crossed the distance between us. I placed my hands on either side of his face. He reached up and traced the angry bruises on my throat. His touch was so gentle it made my stomach twist. I managed a small smile.

'Ah, Calico,' I whispered. 'I came to sea with you, didn't I?'

35

BONNY

We pulled away from Nassau, and New Providence Island, sailing east for the intricate network of Bahamian islands. The wet season was ending. The waters calmed and the days became long and mild. The ocean was so clear you could pick the reefs and dips from the shore. The sand was scorching and white. In the space of a few short weeks the islands of the Bahamas and beyond had changed beyond recognition. The storm-wrecked coasts were now pockets of beauty and quiet. We stopped several times at small islands to take in supplies and give the men time to rest. They all needed it. Usually when we stopped at islands there was drinking, dancing, ribald stories and songs. Now we were quieter. The lads sat by one another and talked, sharing food and tending each other's hurts. We paid locals to keep out of our affairs. They were happy enough to let us rest on their shores, so long as we bought some of their wares and didn't bother them.

We also robbed some fishermen along the coast of Eleuthera because we needed the fishing supplies. Just the necessities. They didn't put up much of a fight and we let them go on their way once we had what we needed.

I sat in the shade with Old Dad. He was skinnier than ever, his beard grown out and his eyes hollow in his dark face. Looking at him I knew he wouldn't be staying with us for long. His days at sea were coming to an end.

'Will you stay on with us until Hispaniola?' I asked him. I handed him a bowl of turtle soup, and was gratified to see he actually started eating. His appetite had been in tatters since the rescue.

'No, boy.' He still called me 'boy', even though he knew I was no such thing. 'I'll step off when we reach Cuba. I got friends there.'

'Who said we're stopping in Cuba?' I asked.

He was sickly, but his eyes were still sharp, glittering. They flicked to me now and treated me with a scornful glare. 'I'm old, not stupid,' he said.

'It's out of our way.'

'You think the captain will pass up a chance to see his son?' He shook his head. 'I know the boy's being raised by the Cunninghams. But that doesn't mean you never see him again. You'll go. For Jack's sake.' He slurped the soup. 'Besides. I won't last until Hispaniola.'

'Dad…'

'You know it's true. The sea's no place for a man with one shot leg. It's a fine ship you've stolen for us, Bonny, but it'll be my coffin if I don't find a place on land soon.'

I didn't know what to say. Old Dad finished his soup and handed me the bowl.

'Don't look at me like that,' he said. 'Sooner or later, every man has to choose where he wants to die.'

'You choose land?'

'I choose a bit of comfort. And a few more years, God willing. Don't you begrudge me that.'

I sighed. 'I don't. But I'll miss you, Dad. There's no one I'd rather plan a murder with.'

He laughed, winced, then laughed again. 'Likewise, Bonny. Likewise.' He reached over and we clasped hands. 'Stay alive, you hear me? I want to hear about you from all corners of the ocean. Make 'em scared.'

He settled back and I let him alone, knowing he'd be asleep soon. When he started to snore I picked myself up and coaxed a mug of beer away from Richard Corner. Then I went down to the beach to find Isaac and Read.

The two men were working together on the beach, lugging wood to replace some small panels on the *William* that had been honeycombed by teredo worm.

True to form, neither of them said anything much but there was an ease between them.

I walked up the beach to join them. 'You're working too hard here, lads.'

'Someone has to,' Isaac muttered. He took a swig from the mug, then handed it to Read. 'How's Old Dad?'

'Sleeping. Seems to have some appetite back so...' I shrugged. 'But he's stepping off in Cuba. Probably for the best.' I rushed on, not wanting to dwell on it. 'Think we can manage the panelling without him?'

'I hope so. If we can't, we're all going to drown.'

Read snorted. 'Ever the optimist, Isaac.'

They traded a smile and I felt, suddenly, like an interloper. I had known the two would be kindred spirits but it hadn't quite occurred to me that there might be more between them.

I fell back a few steps, giving them the option of going on without me. It was Isaac who looked back at me, lifting an eyebrow.

'Don't leave us to do all the work, Bonny,' he said. 'Just because you're sleeping with the captain, doesn't mean you get to shirk.'

We worked through the afternoon. Old shadows and fears were long gone now, replaced with hours of sunlit work and rough jests. It was done with, just another part of our shared past. The ocean was in front of us, and it washed away the lines drawn in the sand.

'Calico.'

It was dark. We had been sailing for over a week and I had spent every night curled against him, matching my breaths with his. I pressed a kiss against his bare shoulder now. He groaned and tried to roll away from me, but the cot in his cabin was small and I was more awake than he was.

'Calico,' I whispered again, snaking my arms about him. 'Wake up.'

'You're killing me, woman.' His voice was slurred with sleep.

'Dobbin just spotted Cuba. We'll be in Havana by dawn.'

'Wake me at dawn then.'

'Calico.' I nipped his ear and he yelped, sitting bolt upright and hitting his head on the roof of the cabin. I cackled and sat up with him. 'Come and stand on the deck with me.'

He glared and tried to drop back into the cot, but I nudged and prodded him until he relented. It was stuffy below decks but the nights had been cool. He slipped on a coat as he followed me up the companionway and into the clear stillness of the upper deck. I breathed in the stiff air off the water and smiled. The *William* was a beautiful craft. She had carried us swift and true to Cuba, responsive and easy. Isaac, used to steering the old *Ranger*, said she was the sweetest vessel he had ever sailed on. I was inclined to agree, though perhaps I was biased. Stolen ships were the easiest to love.

We went to the side and stood leaning on the rail. It was still a strange thing to lace my fingers through Calico's, right out there on the deck. To let my shoulder lean against his without subterfuge. Sometimes the crew would make fun of us, whistling and calling out, but that seemed to have lost most of its novelty by now. So we could stand in one another's company, comfortable and quiet.

The lights of Havana greeted us. They winked and waved with each breath of wind. Somewhere among them I knew our son was sleeping. I let the sadness rest in my ribcage for a moment before letting it go. He would have a good life with the Cunninghams. And, as Old Dad said, we could still see him sometimes. Carefully; no more than once or twice a year.

'What are you thinking?' Calico asked. He had complained enough in the cabin but when I looked at him his eyes were closed and his head was tipped back. Enjoying the breeze and the sound of the waves against our slender vessel.

God, I loved him.

'I'm thinking it's time we started building a fleet,' I said.

He blinked, startled. 'A what?'

'A fleet. Now the business with Barnet is over, we need to make up for lost time. Pirates like Bartholomew Roberts are putting us to shame.'

'Why don't we focus on *keeping* the one ship we actually have?'

'Sure. But I also want a fleet, Calico.'

He stared at me, helpless, then gave a burst of laughter. 'God in Heaven, Annie. Is there anything on this ocean you *don't* want?'

I smiled. 'If I think of something, I'll tell you.'

He took off his coat and dropped it around my shoulders to keep the night chill away. Then he wrapped his arms about me and rested his chin on the top of my head. We fit together well. And we would spend some weeks together in Cuba, just fitting together. We would see our son, talk to the Cunninghams, do right by Old Dad.

When we came back to sea again we would come back with guns and powder and sharpened swords. Taking what we needed and what we wanted. We were the crew of the *William*. We were Calico Jack's people.

I wanted the whole ocean to be afraid.

This is a work of historical fiction, and when it comes to Anne Bonny and her lads there is some difficulty sorting the historical *from* the fiction. There are real and imagined characters in this book, and both real and imagined events. Still, I have done my best to keep my pirates and their enemies aligned with the lifestyles, ideals, personalities, morals (or lack thereof) and bonds that shine through in the historical accounts.

If you would like to know more about Bonny and Read, I would direct you to the first real book that examined their lives and kept them so firmly lodged in the history and mythology of pirates and seafaring:

A General History of Pirates by Captain Charles Johnson. While this is the most complete contemporary source we have on Anne and her people, it should be noted that almost every account of her life, including this one, is filled with sensationalism, mysteries, inconsistencies, rumours and outright lies.

I think she'd like it that way.

ACKNOWLEDGMENTS

Writing this book has made me almost intolerable as a person, but there is a truly ridiculous list of people spanning three continents who have helped and loved and encouraged me all the same. As usual there's no way to thank them all. Consider this my best attempt:

To Mum and Dad, for long days and nights of editing, countless cups of tea, and for always being there; and to my brothers, Ben, Danny and Joe, who take such good care of their dorky sister.

To the team at Text Publishing, especially the wonderful Mandy Brett who saw right to the heart of this book and what it needed to be. Thanks as well to

Jessica Horrocks, who designed a cover any pirate would be proud to sport, and to Simon Barnard for mapping out Anne's world.

To Richard Moore, my excellent sensitivity reader for LGBTQ+ representation. Your patience and practical advice have been invaluable.

To the historians and curators who gave so freely of their time: David Cordingly, for his excellent body of works on pirates and for so kindly meeting with me to help with my research for this book; Eric Lavender and the staff at the Powder Magazine in Charleston (bless you for running a two-hour tour for just me and two other people, even in pouring rain); Pieter van der Merwe, the last remaining defence against institutional stupidity (thank you for answering my inane questions about ship toilets); the staff of the Greenwich Maritime Museum, the Pompey Museum of Slavery and Emancipation, and the National Archives in Kew; Christopher Curry and his daughter Chrisselle who told me all about the pirates of Nassau; Danijela Kambaskovic-Schwartz, my honours supervisor; and Mike Lefroy and the crew of the *Duyfken*, who showed me around their wonderful ship at the very beginning of my research.

Thanks to the numerous taxi drivers, boatmen, sailors, security guards (especially Mister Pinnock), hotel staff and volunteers in Charleston, Nassau and London, who told me their pirate theories and stories, offered local knowledge and advice, and prevented me from getting lost or murdered. And, back home, thanks to the members of SCBWI West and KSP, who take such good care of each other. When the words don't work it's amazing to have a strong community at our backs.

To Peter and Pat Felton, who let me drag them all over England in search of ships, recorded countless documentaries, and sent me pages of research and notes; and to Joan and John Caddy for their support and love. Also thanks to my cousins, Jessica and Elinor Caddy: for book crawls, tea and crafternoons. Please do not send me pictures of shirtless pirates.

To Beverly Twomey, my online writing buddy, who let me drag her all around Charleston and shared a boat with me for a week. Thank you for standing guard (and taking photos) while I trespassed on private property. Please stop making pirate puns.

To Kristin Lane, who drove us all around Charleston and Florida, found me old maps, organised our itinerary around my research and shamelessly encouraged my pirate obsession. Your snark and friendship are lifegiving. Thanks also to Mama and Papa Lane, Caitlin Lane and Noelle Lane, my American family.

To Amb'r and the team at Hay Street, the staff and girls at the Perth College Boarding House, and to Bek Warnes, Maddy Hermawan and Gemma Goepel.

Finally, to my Dungeons and Dragons party: Bridget, Hope, Michael, Nicholas, Serena; and last but never least, Jenn, my sister-in-arms. No context, no mercy. I love you guys.